McCracken
and the
Lost City

With a banshee scream, a cannon ball shrieked over the boat. Instinctively, I ducked. The ball landed with a splash just a few yards on the further side of the boat. A plume of water rose from the sea, and waves expanded outwards from the impact. One of the waves caught the boat and rocked it as if a hurricane had hit us; and I was tipped over the side.

I hit the sea with a splash, and immediately panicked as the water rose over my head. I thrashed about with my hands and feet, which moved slowly and ponderously around me. For a few moments, I couldn't tell which way was up. Then, all at once, my fingertips touched something soft—the sand of the seabed.

Slowly, my eyes grew accustomed to being underwater. Shapes resolved themselves around me.

And the first things I saw were the dead eyes and humourless grin of a shark, hurtling towards me at top speed . . .

Also by Mark Adderley

The Hawk and the Wolf
The Hawk and the Cup
The Hawk and the Huntress
The Heroes of Annwn

For Young Readers:
McCracken and the Lost Island
McCracken and the Lost Valley
McCracken and the Lost Lagoon (forthcoming)

McCracken
and the
Lost City

By Mark Adderley

Scriptorium
Press
Yankton, South Dakota
2014

Published by Scriptorium Press,
Yankton, South Dakota

To Nancy Llewellyn

Contents

CHAPTER 1
A DANGEROUS PURSUIT

The door gave a soft click behind us, and we found ourselves in a darkened room. The sounds of Broadway Avenue, New York City, came to us, soft and muted, through the closed window. We had come to visit the famous inventor, Nikola Tesla, in his office in the Woolworth Building, but I could sense that there were more people in the room than just the wiry Serbian genius.

I began to wonder if we were in trouble.

Another soft click behind us switched on the electric light overhead. The light glinted off the muzzles of the Lugers, and then I knew we were in trouble.

Behind Tesla's desk sat a thin man in a neat suit, but it was not Tesla. His eyes were sunken in his pale face, so that circular shadows gathered around them. Pale, greyish hands lay on the desk in front of him. Between his hands was Tesla's latest invention, the electromagnetic oscillator, the earthquake machine, capable of reducing a whole city block to rubble in moments. All it needed to be fully operational was a narrow filament of wolframite.

My friends and I—my wife Ariadne, Fritz our German servant, Nicolas Jaubert the famous undersea expert—had just liberated a chunk of wolframite from the peak of a mountain in the Yukon and, with much travail and danger, brought it back to New York. It was in the carpet bag I clutched in my right hand.

On reflection, trouble didn't even begin to describe our present predicament.

"Well, Skelett," I said, "nice to see you again. How did you escape from the Caribou People?"

Skelett didn't have any lips, but the shark's slit of a mouth widened into what I suppose he considered a smile. "Herr McCracken," he said, "how I and my colleagues" (he waved an idle hand around at the three others in the room with him: one, I knew, was called Damlich, and I had not long ago thrown him from the roof of a train; the others I couldn't name) "how we escaped from those savages can hardly be any concern of yours. In any case, time presses upon us." He consulted a watch he drew from his waistcoat pocket. "Our steamship departs from Pier 54 in less than two hours."

My eyebrows pressed together. "Pier 54," I said. "White Star or Cunard. One has a reputation for speed, the other for safety. Which do you prefer?"

The smile didn't leave Skelett's face. "This game we have played for many months, Herr McCracken," he said. "The game of witty repartee in situations of

2

extreme danger. I think I shall finish the game now."
He held out his hand, palm-upwards. "The wolframite, if you please."

"Don't give it to him, Mac," said Ari, from beside me.

"Frau McCracken," said Skelett, turning those
dead eyes on her, "he can hardly refuse."

One of the nameless German goons stepped up
behind me. I heard some struggling and muffled
grunts, and knew that they had tied Tesla up and
gagged him. The goon reached out, took the carpet
bag from my hand, weighed it in his own briefly, and
placed it on the desk in front of his boss. Skelett un-
fastened the carpet bag, reached inside, and took out
my Webley revolver and a fragment of cold black
stone. It flashed and sparkled under the electric
light, but its heart was dark and mysterious, as always.

Skelett's goons were close behind us. I could
feel, rather than see, the barrels of the Lugers trained
on us. I started counting: two of them, plus Damlich
and Skelett—four in all, and four of us. Would a
struggle be worth it?

"*Ja, ja*," said Skelett, "I know what it is you think,
Herr McCracken. Casualties there will be, but they
are acceptable. However, let me assure you of one
thing—the first person to die, should you resist, will
be your wife. And we will take her with us to Pier 54

as . . . mmm, how would you say? . . . insurance? A guarantee, anyway, that you will not follow us."

Damlich gave a hoarse laugh as one of the goons stepped forward and frisked Ari. I clenched my fists so hard I could feel the nails biting into my palms, but I could do nothing. The goon reached into Ari's pocket and drew out a revolver, which he tossed over to Skelett. Then he took Fritz's Luger and Jaubert's diver's knife. They made a nice collection of weapons beside the earthquake machine on Tesla's desk. One of the goons had Ari firmly by the arm. He pulled her towards the door.

"I love you," I said.

Ari nodded. "Pray for me," she replied.

Skelett rose to his feet. "Ach, these old-fashioned notions." He made a movement towards us, and the goon yanked our hands behind us, securing them with rough cords. "Always, you must ask for the help of your God. Why? My god is my own will—he has never let me down yet." The goon behind me pulled on the cords and drove me into a wooden chair. "*Ach, gut!*" exclaimed Skelett. He gave a curt bow, snapping his heels together. "*Auf Wiedersehen, Herr McCracken und Freunde.*"

Fritz, his strange eyes lowing with hostility, said something in German that caused Skelett to cock an eyebrow. Ari said, "Thank you, Fritz, but there's no need to be uncivil. I'll see you soon. You'll come right away, love?" she said, as the Germans began to haul her out of the room.

We turned our heads towards her, the chairs' feet rasping on the floorboards. The cords bit into my wrists. "Of course, my dear," I said, "just as soon as I can untie these ropes. I'll see you then."

And she was gone, the Germans with her.

"Herr Skelett should not have told us where he was going," observed Fritz, struggling with his bonds.

"Pier 54!" said Jaubert, with a trace of Gallic triumph in his voice. "*Ma foi*, Monsieur Skelett was unwise to reveal his destination!"

"Heaven reveals the plans of the wicked for the profit of the good," I observed.

Jaubert's brow creased. "Is that—how you say?—a quotation, McCracken?"

"Yes—McCracken, May 1915," I replied. "Or it might be a psalm. I can't remember. Tesla, do you have a gun in here anywhere?"

"Mmmf-hmmm-ffff," replied Tesla, and I remembered he was gagged.

"All right then, it's a relatively simple matter of getting out of these bonds," I said.

My cogitations were interrupted by a loud electrical whirring sound. I turned my head, and saw that one of Tesla's machines, all brass wheels and copper coils, was trundling over the floorboards. It was about the size of a spaniel, and it rolled along on caterpillar tracks. Blue sparks flashed between a pair of aerials that protruded at angles from the top. It was heading straight for the desk and, as I watched, struck it with a loud thud. Everything on the desktop jumped half an inch. The contraption—whatever it was—backed up and then rolled full-tilt into the desk again. A paper knife fell off and clattered on the floor.

In a moment, I saw my chance, and rocked my chair so that it fell over. I landed on my arm, which was immensely painful, but I offered it up, and used my feet to push myself along the floor until I was over the paper knife.

It wasn't very sharp, and I couldn't bear down on the cords very easily. Minutes passed, Tesla's big round wall clock marking the passage of each one as I struggled, more and more frantically, with the knife. Its dull blade scraped back and forth ineffectively over the twisted hemp.

"When we get out of this," I grunted, "I'll make sure I always carry a sharp knife, a dirk or something, in my boot."

"Allow me, Herr McCracken." With a thud, Fritz toppled himself and wiggled over to help me. Back-to-back, we struggled with the paper knife. I glanced up at the clock. Twenty minutes already! I could hardly believe it. The trip to the pier was not a long one, but they would surely be boarding by now.

I felt the cords slacken and, pulling my wrists apart, the ropes fall to the floor. I quickly untied my ankles, then turned my attention to Fritz. He was free in moments. The first thing I did for Tesla was untie his gag. He gasped.

"How did you do that?" I asked as I untied his wrists.

"Those Germans," he said scornfully, "they do not think. How can they expect to surprise an inventor?" He raised a now-released hand, which held a strange metal box with copper coils and a shiny aerial. "I call it remote control—patent number 613809." He gave a wistful half-grin. "I thought we could wage war by remote control, instead of risking lives."

I looked over at the strange contraption that had nudged the desk. A larger version, equipped with a gun—I could see it, in my mind's eye.

But now was not the time. We were all free now, and stood in the middle of Tesla's office, rubbing our wrists.

"Let's go," I said; but Tesla stopped us. For a few seconds, he bustled about his office, collecting various implements of various sinister shapes. He found a hand-gun for me and a Luger for Fritz, a huge knife, almost a machete, for Jaubert, and a long metal stick surrounded by copper coils for half its length for himself. He grinned and, pressing a hidden button in the handle, sent blue sparks flying from the end.

"It is just a cattle prod," he explained with determination, "but it will be perhaps effective. Now, I think, we are ready." And we hurried out of the door and into the corridor beyond.

The Woolworth Building is the tallest building in New York City—in the world, in fact—a great, elongated structure like a Gothic cathedral, reaching sixty stories towards the dazzling sky. The trip in the lift (they call it an *elevator* in America) seemed to take for ever. With a jolt, we reached the ground floor and rushed out through the high-vaulted lobby and emerged, blinking, onto the New York street, bright with the fresh light of the early May morning.

"How do we get there?" I wondered.

"In New York?" said Tesla. "Is easy!" He reached out and snapped his fingers. A black motorcar slowed to a stop beside the pavement (or *sidewalk*, as Americans say). Tesla threw open the door and we all squashed into the back seat of the taxicab.

"Pier 54," Tesla told the driver, and we were off. He pulled out a pocket-watch and consulted it. "We have about sixty minutes until the steamer leaves," he observed. He peered out of the window. "Driver," he said, "why are you going this way?"

"Street market today on 25th Street—it's closed to traffic," replied the driver. The cab jolted along the street. Outside, the tenements and store-fronts rattled past. They were the giant pistons of the civilized world, the people multi-coloured ball-bearings moving in and among them.

"Almost there," remarked Tesla, delving into his pocket. Outside was the entrance to the pier: a tall archway, mostly glass, with doors at the foot. An awning stretched out across the wide pavement, like that of a fancy hotel. Over the awning stood the words WHITE STAR – CUNARD. Other taxi-cabs were drawn up in front and our cabby couldn't park close to the kerb. Tesla dropped a few coins into his palm as we leaped out and into the sunshine. "Keep change," he said, but didn't stay for the profuse thanks of the cabby. The deep bass note of the steamer's whistle blasted out over our heads, though from this angle I could not see her at all.

"Hey, that sounds like final boarding," called the cabby. "You'd better hurry, pal."

In front of me was a photographer, who had one of those motion-picture cameras on a tripod. He was filming the passengers arriving at the pier, and one of them stopped to say, "I'll see this picture when I get to London!" I pushed between them, rushed well ahead of my friends into the building, and stared up at a clock.

Almost immediately, I felt my feet leave the ground. I was moving backwards, my upper arms seized tightly. Something hard and cold and flat pressed against my back—the wall of the pier building.

"You will please not to move, Herr McCracken," said an accented voice in my ear. Two of Skelett's goons had me by the arms.

Damlich approached. He held Ari in one hand; the other was in his pocket, but I could tell from the shape of the bulge that he held a Luger in it.

"Skelett's on board," said Ari, "with the earthquake machine and the wolframite."

"I would have guessed it," I answered.

Damlich turned and treated me to a sneering grin. "You have failed, Herr McCracken," he said. "One week from now, Herr Skelett will have completed the earthquake machine!"

But before he could gloat any more, one of the goons holding me cried out in pain and let me go. I heard a sizzling sound and smelled ozone and burning flesh.

"*Gott im Himmel!*" shouted other the German, springing away from me. Blue flame jumped from Tesla's cattle prod and pierced him between the shoulder blades. He yelled and fell flat on his face.

Damlich backed away from us. "You cannot win, Herr McCracken," he said. "Soon the naval dockyard at Liverpool will be a pile of rubble. And this will be only the first. The Imperial German Army will make many such attacks. No longer can you Englanders hope to win the War!" Damlich smiled in my face. "Enjoy your defeat, Herr McCracken," he sneered.

"*Sacré Bleu!*" gasped Jaubert. "So that is their fiendish plot—Liverpool!"

"*Ich habe eine klare Schuss*, Herr McCracken," said Fritz with earnest menace.

"We haven't time, Fritz," I said. "In English, please."

"He says he has a clear shot, dear," replied Ari. Damlich realized what was going on, and hauled on Ari. The crowd engulfed them again as they moved off towards the dock.

I dived after her, Fritz, Jaubert and Tesla at my heels. Out in the sunshine again, we found ourselves on the wharf, the massive black side of the steamship towering over us. I saw it over a sea of straw hats and feathers and waving hands. The rails were lined with cheering passengers.

"The flag's been raised!" cried someone; and I saw that two white flags fluttered over the bridge. I shouldered my way into the crowd. Cheering surrounded me, the air throbbing with it.

"Isn't that Elbert Hubbard?" asked someone in the crowd. "You know, the author?" He pointed at a figure on the top deck, waving a handkerchief. The whistle blew again, its baritone drowning all the excited chatter.

The whistle died out, and I heard distinctly, "Mac!" I charged after the sound.

"I say, watch out!" someone shouted crossly, as I elbowed him aside.

Damlich stood on the very edge of the wharf, Ari still in one hand. Above them, the sharp prow of the ship rose like one of New York's famous skyscrapers. And there, leaning on the railing and smiling humourlessly, was Skelett. He waved.

Damlich shouted out to me: "Do not move, Herr McCracken, until the boat is gone, or else I will your wife into the water throw."

Once the ship started moving, I knew, there would be a terrible undertow; Ari could hardly be expected to escape that.

"We are four, and he is one," snarled Fritz, who had remembered his English now. He held up the Luger. "And I am sure I can get Herr Skelett."

Seeing Fritz's movement, Damlich panicked, drew his gun, and aimed it at Ari. With great presence of mind, she winked at me, then went totally limp, as if she had fainted, dragging the German down with her. Fritz hesitated a fraction of a second. The barrel wavered from Skelett to Damlich; then it dropped, and the muzzle flashed. Damlich flew over backwards and disappeared from the wharf.

But he pulled Ari with him. She screamed, and there was a splash.

Somebody pushed past me, and I saw the heels of his shoes as he dived over the side of the wharf after Ari. It was Jaubert.

With one last triumphant blast of the whistle, the massive ocean liner began to slide away from the pier. I dashed over to the side of the wharf, already shrugging off my coat. I looked over the edge. Two faces stared back at me, pale amid the seething brown waters: Jaubert and Ari. Jaubert had hold of some steps, while the waters swirled around the two of them, churning and frothing as thirty-two thousand tons of steel, wood, and humanity slipped away from the pier and towards the open sea. The huge displacement caused the waters by the pier to seethe and whirl about, as if some beast below the surface were greedily sucking it in.

More people had noticed now that there was an emergency on Pier 54, and a crowd was gathering. I threaded through them and dashed down the steps. They were slick, and my feet slipped. I reached out and grasped the iron railing, dropped to my backside, and bumped down a few steps. Above me, the crowd gasped, then cheered to see me on my feet again.

Now I was close to Ari and Jaubert. I crouched down and reached out, my fingers stretching towards my wife and my friend. Jaubert struggled against the immense power of the waters, pushing Ari towards me. She reached out. Our fingers met. They closed about one another, and I pulled her in. Her hand scrabbled against the lower steps and, for a moment, I thought she would slip back into the

13

whirlpool that sucked on her legs. But seconds later she had found traction, and hauled herself up the steps to safety. I reached out for Jaubert.

Behind me, I heard Tesla's voice as he assisted Ari up the top half of the steps. I stretched out with my hand, but Jaubert was just too far away.

One more step, I thought.

The water eddied about my knees. The huge tonnage of the steamer was pulling it like some superhuman tide and, for a moment, surprised by its force, I could do nothing but hold onto the railing. Then I prayed, steadied myself, and reached out again. Jaubert's fingers were inches from my own. I took another step down. The filthy waters rose above my waist, and a wave dashed into my face, filling my mouth and eyes. I choked.

"*Ave Maria, Stella Maris!*" Jaubert shouted. A wave slapped him in the face. "*Ora pro nobis!*" The current dragged his feet from under him and he disappeared for a moment.

"Jaubert!" I cried. The liner's whistle blasted again. I strained myself forward.

His hand appeared first, then his face. I stretched out and grabbed his hand. His fingers wrapped about mine, and I heaved on him. And Fritz was there to catch us. We slipped and slid up the steps and back to the pier, entering a mad throng, all cheering.

The cheering, I realized, was not for the steam-ship's departure, but for us.

The crowd closed in on us, shouting with joy, slapping our backs. They had just seen a valiant rescue.

They didn't realize that Damlich had not come back. I looked across at Jaubert. "Damlich?" I said.

He shrugged. "*Requiescat in pace*," he said, and made the Sign of the Cross.

"Herr McCracken," said Fritz, "the German—in the shoulder I shot him. I did not kill him."

Ari had a long greatcoat about her shoulders, and somebody else handed me my own coat. I said, "It must have been the ship's wake that got him, Fritz—you did the right thing to save Mrs. McCracken. Did you get Skelett?"

"*Nein*, Herr McCracken," replied Fritz, frowning. "This Luger—she jammed. I must get a different gun."

"But, McCracken," said Tesla, "the wolframite, the earthquake machine. They are both on that ship."

A valiant rescue, all right, but it was with a sense of utter defeat that I watched the ocean liner slip away from Pier 54. Behind me, a clock was tolling the stroke of twelve noon.

"Well," said someone, "there goes the *Lusitania* once more! How many trips is that?"

15

Somebody else answered, "Two hundred and two—what a magnificent lady she is!"

And I went over to hug my wife. We squelched as we did so.

Chapter 2
A Meeting in New York

Of course, everyone knows what happened to the *Lusitania*. A little less than a week after setting sail, just off the coast of Ireland, a German U-boat torpedoed her. The captain of the submarine had a very lucky shot—a second explosion, moments after the torpedo-strike, blasted a hole in her so big that she sank in twenty minutes, taking with her thirteen hundred passengers and crew. It was a disaster on the level of the *Titanic*, three years previously.

We found out about it from the newspaper reports. We had all gathered in the Manhattan penthouse of Ari's parents, where we were staying until we could get passage back to England.

"The second explosion," Jaubert remarked, scrutinizing the report in the *New York Times*, "was near the bows."

Tesla gave a sigh and shifted in his armchair. He looked out over the roof-tops and skyscrapers of New York City under the bright May sky—a peaceful scene, when turmoil and devastation tore apart so much of the rest of the world.

"Probably the torpedo strike caused an explosion in one of the boilers," I said.

Tesla looked around and, to my surprise, I saw that tears had gathered in his eyes. "Unless," he said, "something else caused the explosion."

I gasped. "You mean the earthquake machine?"

"We will never find out now," replied Tesla, and turned his face back towards the city. I could see from his reflection in the window that he was agitated. Ari glanced quickly at me, then crossed the room and put an arm about his shoulders.

I took the newspaper from Jaubert and scanned the lower half of the article. "The Germans allege that the *Lusitania* was carrying weapons for the Allied war effort," I said. "Bullets and rifles for England made in American factories."

"Perhaps they account for the second explosion," offered Jaubert.

"Unlikely," I said. "Bullets wouldn't explode the way it's described here."

Tesla got to his feet. "Gentlemen," he said, "and madam, this is a terrible day. I fear this act will bring America into the War. But I, for one, will never again make the earthquake machine. If it is true that my invention caused the second explosion, then I am responsible for the ship sinking so fast, and I . . . " His voice broke off and he sank back into the armchair, covering his face with his hands.

"Nikola," said Ari soothingly, "you must pray for them. We can't undo what's been done. But we can pray for them—for the dead, and for the survivors."

"I was trying to do good," said Tesla plaintively. "I was trying to do something that would make this terrible War end quickly. This I never foresaw." He looked up at us, a bleak expression in his eyes. "I wish this dreadful War were over," he said. Taking a deep breath, he got once more to his feet. "I must invent something more useful—something that would make war obsolete. In fact, I shall dedicate my life to it, if my creditors and the U. S. Government will allow me." He shook hands with each of us in turn, and then left.

"He's right," I said, when the front door had clicked behind him. "I knew—my friends and I knew, long ago—that this would be the war of chemicals and engineers. I thought we could invent something that would finish it off quickly, but all we can do is invent things—other people have to use them. And that just means more death." I dropped into Tesla's armchair and stared out of the window, but I could see nothing.

Ari's eyes narrowed. "We have to do our best, love, and pray for the outcome—it's in God's hands, not ours."

"Thirteen hundred souls," I exclaimed, striking the newspaper with the back of my hand. "That could have been prevented—it *should* have been prevented! If it was the earthquake machine that caused the second explosion, then Tesla and I should have prevented it."

I would have said a lot more, but at that moment the doorbell rang. Fritz hurried out into the hallway, and returned a moment later with a small oblong of stiff paper, which he handed me. It was a calling card, imprinted simply with a name in block capitals: JOHN WILMER.

"What does Mr. Wilmer want, Fritz?" I asked.

Fritz shrugged. "He is in the hallway, Herr McCracken. Shall I show him in?"

I nodded. "Perhaps I should leave," said Jaubert, half-rising from his chair.

"No, Nicolas," said Ari. "You were going to stay for lunch. I doubt if this business will take long."

"I'm surprised you need lunch," I observed. "Scrambled eggs at midnight—a bit strange."

"I was hungry," protested Ari.

The door opened, and a dapper gentleman entered. Wilmer was a little shorter than I, of a slight build and a round, clean-shaven and boyish face. He wore a white suit and, when he removed the fedora with the black band, revealed sandy hair. His eye alighted on a picture on the wall, and trouble darkened his brow for a split second. The picture was slightly askew.

"A beautiful picture," he said, his accent a somewhat bland American. "Is that New Mexico?"

"My parents' ranch," explained Ari.

"What a lovely place!" He reached out, as if admiring the picture, and shifted it slightly. Then he turned to us, his even teeth showing in a wide smile. He held out his hand towards me. "Hi. My name's Wilmer, John Wilmer."

"I guessed that," I said, holding up the card. "This is my wife Ariadne, this is our friend Nicolas Jaubert. Won't you sit down?" He lowered himself carefully into a chair by the cold fireplace and smoothed out his trousers. "Would you care for a drink?" I asked.

"Perhaps a small iced tea," Wilmer replied, and I sent Fritz to make them all round.

"What can we do for you, Mr. Wilmer?" asked Ari.

Wilmer smoothed out the velvet of his arm-rest so that all the nap was going in the same direction. "I have some news, Mr. McCracken, that I think will be quite exciting and welcome to you."

"Really?"

"Yes, I think so." Wilmer's blue eyes glinted with good humour. I thought of Skelett's dead eyes, and couldn't help seeing a wide contrast. I smiled back. "I represent someone who's been looking for you for several weeks now," Wilmer went on. "He was unable to locate you until someone close to him read a newspaper report about the daring rescue of a drowning woman while the *Lusitania* was leaving Pier 54 a week ago." He turned his smile on Ari. "Would the drowning woman be you, ma'am?"

Ari nodded. A little surprised, I said, "That made the papers, did it?"

"It sure did," answered Wilmer, "and very exciting reading it was—very stimulating, though recent events have put it in the background a little." He waved a finger at the newspaper, folded up on the coffee table. The headline about the sinking of the *Lusitania* was plainly visible.

"A shocking business," commented Jaubert. "The Boche will pay for it, doubt it not, Monsieur Wilmer."

"Terrible," I said. "Who is this person who's been looking for me?"

Wilmer held out a hand. "Oh, please don't be suspicious, Mr. McCracken. This is a person for whom you have a great deal of friendly feeling, as well as professional esteem."

We didn't find out who it was, however, for Wilmer was interrupted by Fritz's return. He distributed iced teas and, with a short bow, left.

"Has he been with you long?" inquired Wilmer, his lips pursed in a smile.

"Fritz? About two years," I said.

"A good man," said Wilmer. He took a sip from his iced tea. "Do you have a coaster?" he asked. Ari found one for him. He took out a handkerchief, wiped the condensation from the bottom of the glass, and set it down on the coaster, before neatly folding up the handkerchief and returning it to the breast pocket of his suit. He said, "The person who has been so busily seeking you, Mr. McCracken, is Professor Oliver Lychfield."

"Professor Lychfield!" I exclaimed with surprise and delight. At a questioning look from Ari, I explained, "Lychfield was a professor of mine at Imperial. He taught mining—a brilliant man, and a good friend too. He left Imperial just before the War—I don't know why."

"Professor Lychfield," said Wilmer, "needs your help with a project he's working on."

"There's not much I wouldn't do for Professor Lychfield," I said. "How is Mrs. Lychfield?"

Wilmer paused for the tiniest fraction of a second. "Mrs. Lychfield stayed behind in England," he said.

"I see." Somehow, the answer made me uncomfortable, but I suppressed my discomfort and asked, "What's his project? And where? Is it anything to do with the International Mining Institute?" I added, to Ari, "He always wanted to start a special mining college in central Europe somewhere—I suppose the War will have slowed progress on that."

Wilmer nodded in agreement. "The reason he left Imperial College," he explained, "was that he was offered a grant to study the mining practices of an ancient civilization in Mexico. Have you heard of the Mayans, by any chance?"

"I've heard of them," Ari volunteered. "They were somewhat like the Aztecs—their civilization consisted of thousands of cities built from stone. They were gifted mathematicians and astronomers. But they left their cities very suddenly, about a thousand years ago. Nobody knows why."

Wilmer smiled, and his eye glinted again. "You see, I knew you'd find this interesting too, Mrs. McCracken. May I call you Ariadne?" Ari nodded. Wilmer reached inside his jacket and took out a piece of paper. He unfolded it, then bent it against the creases so it would lie flat. In fact, it was a photograph, taken from an aeroplane. It showed what looked like a dense forest, out of which rose a couple of stone structures like pyramids, except that they had steps going up the sides. One of them had what looked like a modern dwelling built at the apex. "This," said Wilmer grandly, "is Xulam-qamtun, a Mayan city about three days' journey south of Campeche, in the Yucatan, Mexico."

"Coolam what?" I said.

"Xulamqamtun," repeated Wilmer.

"It's simple, dear," said Ari, transforming on the spot into a professor of linguistics, "it's pronounced *hoo-lam-kam-toon*. It's a fairly simple Mesoamerican word, like Quetzalcoatl or Tenoxtitlan."

"Hoom-koom-a-loom-boom?" I said.

"Never mind, dear," said Ari, kissing me on the nose. "Let me do the talking." Turning to Wilmer, she asked, "What is there at Xulamqamtun?" pronouncing the word perfectly—confound her.

"Well, frankly, ancient Mayan mines," said Wilmer. "Xulamqamtun seems to have been the heart of the Mayan gold and silver mining industry."

"What does the Mexican government have to say about an English professor exploring Mexican goldmines?" I asked.

"That depends," replied Wilmer. "Which government? There's a revolution in Mexico right now. Xulamqamtun is fairly close to the Gulf of Mexico. You can't see it from the ruins, but the ground all around is waterlogged. Our operation has shut down because of the flooding. That's where you come in, Mr. McCracken. Professor Lychfield heard of your work on the portable water turbine, and said, 'That's the man we need to clear the way through to the lower shafts.'"

I spread my hands. "I'd love to help," I said, "but my turbines are on board my airship, the LS-3, and that's in the Ukraine for repairs."

"Of course," smiled Wilmer. "But we have a fully equipped workshop at Xulamqamtun. I think you'll find our facilities first-rate—more than adequate for building a few more turbines." He took out his handkerchief to mop his brow—it was a little warm in the penthouse—but hesitated. "My handkerchief's a little damp, I'm afraid," he observed. Ari found him one in a sideboard and handed it to him.

"Thank you, Mrs.—Ariadne," he smiled up at her. He dabbed his forehead as Ari opened a couple of windows. The through-breeze cooled us down a little. "What do you think, Mr. McCracken? Will you help us?"

I looked across at Ari, who gave a tiny shrug. It occurred to me that the shrug was meant to convey reluctance, but I stifled my first impression. "You just want me to build a few water turbines?" I asked.

"That's right, and train our people to use them," replied Wilmer. "You'll be working with Mr. Dean, our on-site engineer." Turning to Ari, he said, "Ariadne, there would be a place for you on this expedition. The locations of the shafts are recorded in pictures on the walls and on standing stones in the pyramids and some of the other buildings."

"Glyphs?" said Ari.

"Yes, glyphs," said Wilmer. "We'd like you to help us decode them, if you would, Ariadne."

"Well," said Ari hesitantly, "I don't know much about the pre-Colombian languages, but I could probably find out a little from some of my old colleagues here in New York."

"Jaubert," I said, "will you come?"

"*Mes apologies, mes amis*," responded Jaubert. "I must leave for Europe at once. I cannot stay in the *Monde Nouveau* any longer. France, she has a need of me."

"You're going back to France?" I asked.

"Ah, *non*," replied Jaubert, "but I cannot say where I will go. It is—how do you say?—top secret."

"But you will come to Xulamqamtun, Mr. McCracken?" asked Wilmer.

"I'd do a lot for Professor Lychfield—I owe him a great deal," I answered.

"Then it's settled." Wilmer rose, straightening his tie. "We can't travel to the Yucatan overland, what with the Revolution in the north. But I can get you on a steamship for tomorrow."

"I'll have to follow in a few days," said Ari. "I have a doctor's appointment, and I have to talk to some of my friends who know the Mayan languages. Could you book me and Fritz on a steamship on, say, next Friday?"

"Very well, Ariadne," replied Wilmer. "Thank you for your help, Mr.—could I use your first name?"

"McCracken will do," I said.

"Thank you very much, Mr. McCracken, Ariadne," said Wilmer, and we rang for Fritz to show him out.

"*Mes amis*," said Jaubert with sudden earnestness, when Wilmer had left, "I must leave soon, but this I must say before I depart: be careful, very careful. This man Wilmer I do not trust."

"You've only just met him!" I protested.

"I kind of agree with Nicolas," said Ari. "He's a little too neat, a little too perfect. I didn't like the way he adjusted that picture of the ranch."

"Well, God forbid he should straighten a crooked picture!" I said. "What was he thinking? He must be a villain—I see it all—an incorrigible picture-straightening villain!"

"Oh, don't be sarcastic," said Ari, her perfect nose wrinkling in a most fetching way. "I've a mind to do a little extra research—not just into the Mesoamerican languages."

"You can't be serious," I said. "I've known Lychfield for years. He's absolutely sound."

Ari took my hands in her own and looked into my eyes. "If you absolutely forbid me to make any inquiries about Professor Lychfield and Mr. Wilmer," she said, "I promise I won't."

"Well, that's ridiculous," I said. "I certainly won't forbid you."

"Good." She reached up and kissed me on the nose. And I knew I'd lost that argument.

CHAPTER 3
A VOYAGE TO MEXICO

Wilmer had got me a first-class ticket on the *Esperanza*, a delightful steamship with twin funnels standing side-by-side behind the bridge, operated by the Ward Line. So after Mass the following morning, Ari, Fritz and I climbed into a taxi-cab and found ourselves covering some of the same route we had taken after the Germans just a week before. The *Esperanza* was due to reach Campeche sometime on Thursday morning.

"Don't forget to wear your hat," said Ari, as we hurried along Pier 17. "The sun will be strong in Mexico—we don't want you getting sunstroke."

"Isn't she a beauty?" I sighed.

"*Jawohl*, Herr McCracken," said Fritz. "Perhaps that is why you married her?"

"I was talking about the ship," I said. Then, noticing Ari's expression, I hurriedly added, "Which is almost as beautiful, in her own way, as my wife." I narrowed my eyes. "I think she was built in Philadelphia."

Fritz cleared his throat. "In New York, surely, Herr McCracken."

"No, look." I pointed. Near the deck was a manufacturer's tile that read WILLIAM CRAMP & SONS SHIPBUILDING, PHILADELPHIA, PENN. "She must be—what?—four and a half thousand gross tons?"

Fritz blinked in confusion. Ari punched me on the shoulder. "You're not going to see me for two whole weeks," she said, "but you'll be on the ship in just a few minutes. Did you pack your revolver?"

"Of course I packed my revolver," I answered, my eye straying towards the gangplank. "I wouldn't leave home without it."

We walked on a little way. "I put some spare ammunition on the night-stand last night," Ari went on. "Did you get it?" I nodded. "Good. Please re-member to brush your teeth, and don't think you can skip your greens just because I'm not with you."

We had reached the gangplank now. "I'd better get on board," I said, apologetically. "Are you going to be all right?" She had felt a little under the weather this morning.

"I'll be fine. A nice, leisurely sea voyage will be just the thing to pick me up, next week." Her eye-brows met in a frown. "Will you get going?" she said. "You'll be late!" I kissed her and squeezed her hand. "God be with you," she said.

"And with you."

"*Auf Wiedersehen*, Herr McCracken." Fritz set down my suitcases and we shook hands. I took up

30

the cases again and strode up the gangplank, handing my ticket to the officer collecting them on the deck.

"'Bye, sweetheart!" called Ari. "I love you!" The last word was overwhelmed by a long bray from the funnel overhead. Looking up, I saw a seaman running the Ward Line's ensign—a W in a black circle on a white pennon—up over the bridge. We were about to depart. I waved down to Ari.

A second seaman hurried past me towards the stern, where he cast off the line while a third repeated the operation in the bows. The tug-boat whistled merrily—I have a very great fondness of tugboats, they're so cheery and fussy—and drew us slowly away from the pier. Ari's face dwindled in the crowd, and I watched her until I could no longer distinguish even her beauty from the faces surrounding her.

We were clear of the wharf now. The whistle blew, the triple-expansion steam engines began to thump, and the *Esperanza* moved away from New York Harbour. We nosed past the Statue of Liberty, resplendent in her copper-green livery. Behind her, I could make out the Woolworth Building among the forest of skyscrapers.

The whistle blew again in farewell, and we headed out to sea, smoke and steam trailing from our funnels.

After depositing my suitcases in my cabin, I went aft and made the acquaintance of the Chief Engineer, a man in his mid-sixties from Maine, who had shoveled coal on a whaler for a couple of decades, and claimed to have met in his youth a man called Ishmael who had seen a white whale.

My cabin seemed to be the largest one on the ship, a whole suite. One room contained two beds and a wardrobe, the other a sofa, armchair, and coffee table. There was a small washroom off the bedroom. The walls were paneled with light wood, and two neat portholes looked out at the New Jersey coastline. Under one of them stood a small desk with a roll top.

So my voyage to Mexico began. For several days, it was uneventful. We plied past the Carolinas, with their piratical history, and along the sun-drenched coast of Florida. Then we turned west. I lost sight of the coast and had to go out on deck to see Cuba sliding past on our port side. I spent most of my time with the old engineer below decks, some in my cabin sharpening my dirk. I'd bought it, true to my promise in Tesla's office, from an antique dealer on the corner of 3rd Street and Court back in New York. He had assured me that the dirk had once belonged to Rob Roy; I could tell it wasn't that old, but I knew it would sharpen to a razor's edge, and so I paid my money and set about restoring it.

One afternoon, when I had been reading Henry T. Brown's *507 Mechanical Movements* for about two hours, it dawned on me that something about the motion and sounds of the ship was different, and it took me a moment to work out what it was.

The engines had stopped.

And just when I had worked that out, the report of a large-calibre gun rattled the glass in my port-holes and the little chandelier over my head.

I jumped to my feet and stared out of the port-hole, but I could see nothing except the blue expanse of the sea. I quickly loaded my revolver and hurried up on deck.

There, lying a hundred yards off our port side, was a long, sleek boat. She was about ninety feet in length, with almost no superstructure except a low deckhouse in the stern. A single funnel rose amidships, two or three feet taller than the helmsman, who stood directly in front of it, his beefy hands dwarfing the handles of the wheel. Deck guns were mounted fore and aft. Both were trained on the *Esperanza*. From the stern fluttered a black flag. The wind tugged at it, and I gasped in amazement.

The flag bore the skull and cross-bones.

I hadn't heard of any pirate activity lately. Who was the captain of this outmoded vessel, styling himself a pirate in this modern world of compound engines and machine guns, rather than sails and flintlocks?

Still, the guns mounted fore and aft were modern enough—three-inch naval guns that looked like U.S. Navy surplus—and they were pointed right at our waterline. Three Vickers machine guns mounted on the near side railing covered our deck.

So many passengers had lined the port rails that the *Esperanza* was listing slightly. I ran quickly up some steps to the bridge, where I accosted Welch, the captain, a leather-skinned old salt with a bushy white beard.

"Is this really a pirate attack, captain?" I asked.

Captain Welch turned to me, a confused expression on his face. "It looks very much like it, McCracken," he said, "though I'm blessed if I can explain it—the U.S. Navy cleared up all pirate activity in the Caribbean well over a century ago."

At that moment, a voice, amplified by a bullhorn, came to us across the waters: "Captain of the passenger vessel *Esperanza*, heave to and prepare to receive boarders!" it said. The accent seemed to be Cuban.

"I don't have any choice," said Captain Welch, spreading his hands. "She's a fast vessel, all right—came right up alongside of us out of nowhere in no time flat. And the *Esperanza*'s unarmed." He picked up his own bullhorn, leaned through a port window and called back: "This is Captain Welch of the Ward Line ship *Esperanza*. Who in God's name are you?"

34

"God's name?" sputtered the Cuban voice. "In God's name, is it? What do you Americans know about God, you faithless Puritans? Heave to or we open fire!"

"With whom have I the pleasure of speaking?" asked Captain Welch.

"I am Capitán Gusta of the privateer *Fortuna de las Serpientes*. Heave to, Capitán Welch, or I open fire!"

"Fortune of Serpents?" I said doubtfully.

"Luck of Snakes," the captain corrected me. "It's not a very good name, is it?"

The *Fortuna* was very close to us now. I could see variously dressed sailors lining the near rails. As they came close, each one of them tossed out a rope with a grappling hook, which rattled on our own rails. They heaved, and the two ships drew close.

"*Me gusta!*" came a booming voice, and Captain Gusta appeared on deck. He wore a blue pea-coat with brass buttons and a white captain's peaked cap. He had slung a scarlet sash from his left shoulder, and he brandished a revolver that flashed as it moved. I couldn't see his face clearly.

Slowly, I reached down to my pocket and drew out my revolver.

"I'd be obliged, McCracken," said Captain Welch, "if you'd not do that. I'd like as little trouble caused for my passengers as possible."

"Of course, sir," I said, returning the revolver to my pocket. "If you'll excuse me." He nodded permission, though he didn't really need to grant it, and I left the bridge.

About a dozen pirates had boarded us by the time I reached the deck, and Gusta himself was climbing on board. Now he was close, I could see that he had the handsome, chiseled features of many Cubans. He wore a narrow moustache with a tiny triangle of beard under his lower lip, but his chin had not been shaven in two or three days. He held a fat Havana cigar between his teeth. There was something familiar about him, but I couldn't quite put my finger on what.

"Felicitations, my dear passengers!" he cried out, his arms wide. "I mean you no harm!" He smiled in a particularly winning way, his teeth bright in the sunburned face. "I do not wish to take from you more than you can afford."

"What do you mean by that, sir?" asked a passenger, a man in his late fifties with white hair and a bushy moustache like Mark Twain's.

Gusta continued to smile. "If you will collect, say, two hundred American dollars' worth of valuables from your fellow passengers, I will be content to steam away and leave you all in peace."

"You wish to steal two hundred dollars from us, sir?" asked the passenger, not quite sure he had heard correctly.

36

"That is not quite correct, *señor*," answered Gusta. "I wish to steal nothing—I wish for you to give it to me. I am no thief."

"Well, that's an interesting distinction," I said drily.

Gusta looked at me, and his eyes became dark slits. He took the cigar from between his teeth. "McCracken?" he said.

Then it hit me: I had met him several years before, in the Amazon. "Felipe?" I said.

"No, *señor*, not Felipe," replied Gusta. "He is my brother—a guide on the Amazon. But we met, I think, before you took that expedition with him." He thrust the cigar back into his mouth and puffed on it a few times.

"Well, it's grand to see you again!" I exclaimed. "How have you been?"

Gusta stepped closer and lowered his voice a little. "Not so well, *señor*," he said confidentially. "Do you think I would be doing this—exacting taxes in this way—if things had been going well?"

"I hadn't thought about it," I admitted. "But, well, two hundred dollars isn't much."

"I calculate," said Gusta, holding the cigar between his first two fingers and doing invisible calculations with it in the air, "that if I stop one ship a week, and take two hundred dollars from each, then by the end of the year, I will have enough money to buy a plantation in Colombia."

"In Colombia?"

"*Si, señor.* A coffee plantation."

"If you two have finished catching up on old times, perhaps you could return your attention to us?" said the passenger who had spoken before.

"Ah, *si, si!*" exclaimed Gusta. "Two hundred dollars—such a small amount is no great hardship, I think." There was some grumbling from the passengers, who began going through their pockets to see what they had. Gusta turned back to me. "What is it you do here, McCracken—do you go all the way to Campeche?"

"Yes, I'm helping a friend work on some Mayan ruins just south of Campeche," I said.

Gusta's thick eyebrows met over his nose. "Xulamqamtun?" he asked.

"Yes, Koomie-hoomie-toon," I said.

Gusta narrowed his eyes again and stared at me for what seemed a very long time. At last, he said, "*Señor,* do you have any obligation to finish your voyage on this ship, or could you go to Campeche by another means, should the notion seem good to you?"

I was confused for a moment. "I don't have to finish my voyage on this ship, I suppose," I said. "What are you suggesting?"

"I think you should come with me on board the *Fortuna de las Serpientes,*" he said. "My apologies, it is not a very good name—I have only just acquired her. But I would be honoured to host you on the *Fortuna*; and I have a few things I would like to tell you about this Xulamqamtun. I think you would find the conversation very interesting."

I hesitated. It was a radical change in plan; and how did I know I could trust this man—this pirate?

Gusta took a long draw on the cigar and blew a cloud of smoke out into the salty air. The wind blew it away at once. "How," he said carefully, "is Father Jamie Erickson these days? Have you seen him recently?"

"Do you know him?" I asked.

"I have not seen him for some years, *señor*," admitted Gusta. "He spoke to me once, at great length, and over many glasses of rum, in a very rough cantina in Lisbon. When I emerged, I was not the same man."

"That sounds like Fr. Jamie, all right," I observed. And that made up my mind. "It would be my pleasure to sail with you to Campeche, Captain Gusta," I said.

"Excellent!" bellowed Gusta. "Tell my men your cabin number—they will fetch your possessions."

"Excuse me, sir," said the passenger. He held a wad of bills in his hands, and a little change. "All we could muster, sir, is one hundred and eighty-four dollars and fifty-four cents. But we could probably raise the difference if we could return a moment to our cabins."

"No no no, *señor*, it is close enough." Gusta scooped the money from his hands and stuffed it into the pocket of his pea-coat. Some pennies rattled on the deck, and a five-dollar bill floated lazily towards the sea. "*Gracias, señor.* Come, McCracken, let us drink and smoke cigars, and talk of many things! How is that beautiful young lady you took with you down the Amazon?"

"She's my wife now," I explained.

"Your wife?" Gusta bellowed with laughter. "That is what my brother said would happen—you are . . . what is the phrase? . . . a lucky dog! She is very beautiful, I think! Be careful—the *Fortuna* moves more in the water than the bigger ship."

And so I finished my voyage to Campeche on board a pirate ship, reflecting on what strange turns my story had already taken.

Chapter 4

A Caribbean Cruise

Gusta threw open the door of the stern deckhouse and stepped aside to allow me to de-
scend the steps into his cabin and office.
We were already steaming away from the *Esperanza*—probably, we were making a little faster than 20
knots.

Gusta's cabin was a bit of a mess. It looked as if
somebody had got part way through demolishing it,
and then had been stopped by someone who had
started rebuilding it in another way but couldn't be
bothered to finish. Exposed electrical wires, copper
pipes and tubes ran along the walls below the windows, the bunk was unmade, and piles of books, papers, and empty glasses lay scattered over the table.
In the forward starboard corner stood a sink with a
mirror over it; in the opposite corner stood a globe;
between them was a desk, littered with papers and
charts, dividers, parallel rulers and a sextant. There
were two sofas. On one of them was a massive atlas,
open at a relatively large-scale map of Colombia. On
the other was a jaguar. It was just a cub, but nevertheless, a jaguar. Its spotted hide contrasted sharply
with the black leather of the sofa. As we entered, it

rolled over on its back and stretched out its white tummy. Grinning, Gusta tickled it a moment.

"This is El Tigre," he said. "Just a little pet I picked up a few weeks ago." He shrugged. "It's not a good name, I know. Hey, you lazy son of a molly, move over and let Señor McCracken sit down, eh?" The jaguar didn't move, but curled up when Gusta moved away. "He doesn't understand English well," Gusta observed. "If I say it in Spanish, he understands, and he will do it. *¡Hi, Tigre! ¡Mueve tu culo peludo! Que el señor McCracken se siente.* Hey, McCracken, you want a glass of rum, eh?"

"That would be lovely," I replied. The door opened behind me, and one of Gusta's men clattered down the steps and set my suitcases on the floor. I'm not quite sure how he found the space. Then he bobbed his head to Gusta and ran back up the steps.

Gusta opened up the globe—it turned out to be hollow—and brought out a bottle, which he set down on his desk. He swilled out a couple of glasses in the sink, dried them, and poured generous measures.

"Sit down, sit down!" he urged me. "Tigre won't mind."

I lowered myself onto the sofa, nudging Tigre gingerly aside as I did so. The rum was good, but I don't know rum like I know whisky.

"You like it, eh?" said Gusta, grinning and gulping his own. He pushed a cigar box towards me, flipping open the lid. "You want a cigar? They are rolled in Havana, my home town."

"Thanks, maybe later," I said.

"Okay, your loss." He blew out a cloud from his own cigar. Already, a blue haze hung around the ceiling. He sat behind his desk and put his rum down on the chart he had been plotting. "Now, to business. Xulamqamtun. What do you know of this place?"

"Not much," I confessed. "A friend of mine, Professor Oliver Lychfield, just discovered it."

"Pah!" Gusta made a dismissive gesture with his hand. Smoke from his cigar wafted back and forth. "That is nothing. These ruins—they are found every day, and forgotten every day. In that jungle, you might be standing ten feet away from Mayan ruins, and know nothing of them. You could dig them out of the jungle, go away for a week, and when you come back, you would not be able to find them. These ruins, they are a common thing. Why do you go there?"

I gave him a brief summary of Wilmer's visit, and described Professor Lychfield, his interests and our friendship. After I had finished, Gusta sat, silent and thoughtful, for a long while, puffing on his cigar and sipping on his rum. At last, he shook his head. "Something about this does not make sense, *mi amigo*," he said. "This Professor Lychfield—do you trust him?"

"Of course," I responded. "I owe him a lot—I learned so much from his lectures."

"That too is nothing," asserted Gusta. "That is merely professional. What was he like as a man? Did he have a family?"

"He had a wife and one son," I said. "She didn't say much, but she was very sweet. They stayed behind in England."

"For two years?" Gusta's shoulders shook briefly in a mirthless laugh. "That is not a very good home life, *mi amigo*. For one thing, he has only one child—that does not suggest he loves his wife very much. And for another, they stayed behind for a very long time. That suggests they do not enjoy spending time with him."

"Well, he was always very busy with his lectures and his research. He was trying to start an International Mining Institute in Europe."

"Worse and worse!" exploded Gusta. "Why does a man, in love only with his work, marry at all?" After a brief pause, he shrugged, refilled his rum, stubbed out his cigar, and topped up my glass. "You can ignore me if you like, *mi amigo*," he said, "but in my experience, when a man spends so much time at work, it is because he is trying to escape."

"From Mrs. Lychfield?" Now I laughed. "That's absurd—she was so sweet, so compliant."

"Perhaps it was not her he was trying to escape—it was himself," suggested Gusta. He held up one hand, palm-outwards. "But do not press me any further, *mi amigo*. I do not know this man. Only you know him well enough to say the kind of things I am saying."

I was a little ruffled by this exchange, and pouted a little. "That's true," I said. "If you knew him as I know him, you'd like him very well indeed. He was always giving his knowledge and his expertise to his students. And they loved him for that. I think he always felt he couldn't give enough—he wanted to give more. That's why he wanted to start the International Mining Institute, to share his knowledge with even more people."

"It is most likely you are correct," returned Gusta. "Still, be careful. Things are not right about Xulamqamtun. I have an *amigo* in Lerma—that is a coastal village just a few miles south of Campeche. Sometimes, he tells me when wealthy ships are leaving Campeche, and where they are bound. Now he tells me the Ququmatz are stirring."

"The Ququmatz?"

"*Si*, the Ququmatz. They are a tribe in the interior of the Yucatan, descendants of the Maya. This *amigo* of mine does not like them. They worship the feathered serpent—in their beliefs, he is the creator of the world. He coughed the sun out of his mouth. Now, they put the sun back into the mouth of the feathered serpent in a ball game called Ollamaliztli. I will not tell you the rules, *mi amigo*—it will give you the *pesadillas*—you know, the bad *sueños*, the stories that come into your head when you sleep, the crazy stuff."

"Dreams?" I said. Beside me, on the couch, Tigre stretched, yawned, and put his head on my lap. I petted him between the ears. "Nightmares?"

"*Sí, sí*—nightmares. That is it, *señor*, it will give you *ni-i-ight-mares*. A few years ago, these Ququmatz, they were just another snake cult—now, it is very sinister indeed."

"Is there anything else?"

"There is," said Gusta. "But this is not scary stuff—and I have seen it myself—a submarine."

"Was it German?"

"Who else would use the submarines? This one, it has U-53 painted on the . . . the thing that sticks up in the middle of the deck."

"The conning tower?"

"*Sí, sí!* Conning tower."

I got up and wandered over to the starboard windows. Tigre looked up lazily at me and then put his head down on the sofa once more. The *Esperanza* was already a mere dot on the horizon. The two facts Gusta had revealed were probably unrelated to what I was doing in Mexico, I reasoned. I turned back to Gusta and said, "I know the Germans are patrolling the Gulf of Mexico."

Gusta nodded. "If you want my opinion, *señor*, the Germans are in trouble. This business with the

Lusitania was a big mistake, a *big* mistake! Many people do not like what they have done. Perhaps, now, the Americans will fight in this War, on the side of the English. But if the Germans can persuade the Mexicans, and especially this troublesome fellow, Pancho Villa, to stir up trouble for the Americans, maybe they will be too busy to fight beside the English, eh?"

"More than anything," I said, "I bet the Germans need money—it costs a lot to finance a war, especially one that depends as much on technology as this one does."

"Hey, who doesn't need money?" replied Gusta. "Look at me—fifth son of a tobacco planter, and what do I have? My oldest *hermano*, Sarín, he went into the Church—he is the black sheep of the family—so my next oldest brother, Manuel, he has the plantation now. My next brother, he is a colonel in the army, or in the Revolution, I forget which. An honourable career, either way. My fourth brother, that is Felipe, he lives in Brazil and guides lunatic Europeans along the Amazon. What is there for me? Nothing. For many years, I sailed around the world on a merchant ship. And at the end of it, was I any richer than at the beginning? No! Where am I to get *my* plantation from? What about my *esposa*? All the little *niños*? How am I to pay for them? So, I went into business on my own."

"Do you think Fr. Jamie would approve of your career choice?" I asked mildly.

He opened his mouth and shut it again with an audible snap. "That is why I have not seen him in many years. When I see him, his penance will be a big one, I think, and then I will have to give up what I am doing now."

"You could confess to your brother," I pointed out.

"Sarín? Yes, he might be more sympathetic, of course—he will understand the pressures under which I have lived. He will be merciful to me, *mi hermano*."

"That's not good theology," I observed.

Gusta's brow clouded a little. "Well, it is the best I can do under the current circumstances," he said. He frowned. "I hope you are not going to nag me?" he asked. "I promise, before Almighty God and His Mother, I will give up the pirate's life once I have the money for my plantation in Colombia." He held up the rum bottle. "Another drink?"

"I'd better not," I said. "The boat's swaying enough for me as it is. Where do I sleep?"

It turned out that Gusta had a pair of hammocks in his cabin, so that he wouldn't need to make his bed, and I swayed gently on the starboard side as I slept that night, Gusta and Tigre snoring softly on the port.

We had been almost at the mid-point between the western end of Cuba and the northernmost tip of the Yucatan when Gusta had intercepted us. That meant almost a day's travel would take us to Campeche, which is just about in the middle of the western coast of the peninsula. So I expected it to be about noon that we would make landfall. I enjoyed the voyage that morning very much indeed. We went fast enough that a breeze blew in our faces, taking the edge off the blistering heat. I did remember to wear my hat, as Ari had insisted.

"What's that?" I asked one of the sailors, as I stood at the forward rail. I pointed at a triangular fin, cutting through the waters perhaps twenty yards from our starboard bow. "Is it a dolphin?"

"That is no dolphin," replied the sailor calmly. "Look at the way he moves, straight through the water, not up and down—that is *el tiburón* . . . what is the word in *Inglés*?"

I gulped a little and said, "A shark?"

"*Si, si!* A *sha-a-ark*," said the sailor, trying out the new word by stretching the vowel.

"Are they man-eaters?" I asked.

The sailor shrugged. "It depends," he said. "If it is a Nicaragua Shark, it will eat a man. If it is a whale shark, no."

"How can you tell which is which?" I asked.

The sailor thought about it for a moment, his eyes narrowing as he stared at the bright water.

Then he leaned closer to me, as if imparting a secret, and said, "Jump in and have a swim, *señor*—if the shark eats you, he was a Nicaragua Shark." He threw back his head and bellowed with laughter.

His laughter was interrupted by a crash of gunfire, which made us both spin around in surprise. Gusta stood at the rail by the helm, a revolver grasped in both hands. He fired into the sea until the hammer clicked on an empty chamber and, with an angry grimace, he returned it to his holster.

"Are you all right?" I asked him.

"It is that thing, that thing!" he cried out, pointing at the shark's dorsal fin, which still cut unimpeded through the sea. "That giant lump of swimming death." Gusta shuddered. "I hate them, hate them all. If you touch their skin the wrong way, it will cut you. If you are in the water when one passes by, you are dead. Not wounded, not scratched—dead. It is they who hunt you, not the other way around, God and all His holy angels protect us! They are worse than lawyers, worse than politicians. Me and the sharks," he concluded, "we do not get along well. Ah!" With a sudden brightness in his face, he pointed. "Mexico!"

I turned to see a ribbon of green stretched out along the horizon. Below it, like a fringe, hung a thin band of intense white—a sandy beach. As we got closer, I could see palm trees inland, and once a flight of flamingos, winging lazily from one side of a lagoon to the other.

"Are we far from Campeche?" I asked.

"Not far," answered Gusta. "Ten miles, fifteen perhaps. My men will put you ashore here—Sarín has his parish nearby. He will help you get to Campeche. We cannot put into such a big port. It would cost way too much to bribe the Harbour Master."

"I'll get my things," I said, and strode back into the cabin to gather my belongings. A few minutes later, I heard the engines slow, and lugged my suitcases up on deck.

When I got there, a couple of sailors were lowering a jolly boat into the water. They took my suitcases and dropped them into it.

"Well, *mi amigo*," said Gusta, striding towards me and throwing open his arms, "*adios!* Find my *hermano*'s parish, and he will help you get to Campeche. I did not steal all of your money, eh?" He laughed heartily. "But something tells me," he added, tapping the side of his nose, "we shall meet again."

"I shall certainly pray for it," I said, shaking his hand. He stuffed a couple of cigars into my breast pocket and laughed.

"Go with God," he said. "I pray that your business at Xulamqamtun will prosper."

I slung myself over the side and climbed down into the jolly boat. Two sailors waited for me. One of them pushed off while the other slipped the oars through the oarlocks and began sculling towards the coast.

Ahead of us was the gentle white slope of the beach and the green tangle of the forest. Seagulls filled the air with their cries. Looking over the gunwale, I could see right to the sandy bottom of the sea, and schools of fish, dark against the sand or sparkling in the sunlight, flitted this way and that. My mind went back to my adventures in Greece, where Jaubert and I had explored the intricate and jungular bed of the Mediterranean Sea.

Something large moved across my line of vision, something bigger than a man, with knife-like fins on either side. I jumped backwards in the boat, and the sailors laughed. *"El tiburón?"* said one of them. I gave them an ironic smile back, then looked over my shoulder to see how much we had gained on the land. Not quite enough, I decided.

It was then that a piercing sound came to us across the waters: the shrill cry of the *Fortuna*'s whistle. My companions stared left and right in alarm.

"Debemos volver a la barco," one of them said urgently, leaning towards me and staring directly in my face.

"What is it?" I asked, half-standing and looking around.

Then I saw it: a boat, perhaps a quarter of a mile off, to the starboard. It looked like a glorified rowing boat, except that it was about fifty feet long, with a funnel in the middle and a cannon mounted in the bows. A Mexican flag streamed from the stern mast.

"*Armada de México,*" snarled one of my companions, as they began to turn the boat in the water. Mexican Navy? I thought. Coast Guard, perhaps?

I saw the muzzle flash a moment before I heard the report. A puff of smoke appeared about the cannon's mouth, and was whisked away almost instantly. With a banshee scream, a cannon ball shrieked overhead. Instinctively, the three of us ducked our heads. The ball landed with a splash just a few yards on the further side of us. A plume of water rose from the sea, and waves expanded outwards from the impact. One of the waves caught our boat and rocked it as if a hurricane had hit us.

And I was tipped over the side and into the shark-infested waters.

CHAPTER 5
TEETH AND BULLETS

I hit the water with a splash, and immediately panicked as the water rose over my head. I thrashed about with my hands and feet, which moved slowly and ponderously around me. For a few moments, I couldn't tell which way was up. Scintillating silvery bubbles surrounded me, but I couldn't tell which way they were going—to me, they just looked like a confused mass. Then, all at once, my fingertips touched something soft—the sand of the seabed.

The bubbles began to dissipate, and my eyes grew accustomed to being underwater. Shapes resolved themselves around me.

And the first things I saw were the dead eyes and humourless grin of a shark. It was hurtling towards me at top speed, upside-down.

Except the shark wasn't upside-down—I was, and the giant lump of swimming death was already gaping wide to snap at my feet.

It takes a long time to tell all this, but really, it all happened in a flash.

I raised my knees up under my chin—down and over my chin, I suppose it was, really. That snatched my feet away from the dreadful scythe-mouth of the shark as it swept by overhead. A wave of cooler water fanned across me. I spun myself around so that I was the right way up and kicked at the seabed, sending up clouds of sand about me.

My chest was hurting now; I hadn't had time, of course, to fill my lungs with air. The shark was a long way off and beginning to turn, but I had a moment, so I returned to the surface of the sea, drew in a deep breath, and plunged once again below the waves.

For a moment, I couldn't sight the shark, and I began to panic. It knew where I was! I spun round and round under the water.

Suddenly, I saw a flash of pink gums and triangular teeth. In my fright, I lashed out with my foot and, by a lucky stroke, kicked the fish on the side of the head—right in the gills. The shark closed its mouth and with a flick of the tail took off in another direction. I returned once more to the surface of the water.

This time, I could see the dorsal fin some yards away. It was turning, cutting through the blue waters, sending up a silver plume on each side.

I hadn't got enough air yet. I tried to remember everything I'd learned, years ago, from that Australian fisherman, about surviving shark attacks. First lesson: keep your eye on the shark. Well, I could see the fin. It wasn't coming towards me. It had failed in a frontal assault, and was now circling me.

No sudden movements, I thought, but try to get to shore as smoothly as possible. I took a few casual strokes towards the land. The shark continued circling me, like a vulture of the sea.

Now I had enough air. With a deep gulp, I dived once again. So far, I hadn't been able to take the offensive—I'd just been trying to breathe and to survive. But now my heart was grim. Lesson two, I recalled: if the shark doesn't swim away, take the offensive by striking at its eyes, snout, or gills.

I torpedoed through the blue world towards the seabed and into a clump of seaweed. I dug my feet into it so that I was as low as I could possibly be. I had no idea what I could do, but I was sure something would come to me.

The shark was making for me once more. Out of the corner of my eye, I could see another grey nightmare, watching warily, its wide tail fanning back and forth. Gusta's words came unbidden to my mind, and I prayed, "God and all His holy angels, help me!"

Then I remembered the dirk from the antique shop in New York, the one that the dealer had insisted had belonged to Rob Roy.

The shark that had already charged me now headed directly for me. I reached to my boot and slid out my dirk. My lungs were beginning to protest again, but I was dead, I knew, if I didn't make an end of things now.

The shark's jaws opened wide. Two rows of teeth seemed to extend out towards me.

If the shark bit me at all, if it so much as scratched my skin, I knew that the blood in the water would incense the other shark as well, and I would be done for. Danger above, and danger below: a no-win situation.

But that was what I was used to.

The shark was almost upon me. Rob Roy's dirk was in my hand.

I pulled on the seaweed and so ducked a whole three feet lower, at the same time thrusting the dirk straight up through the waters. The shark's jaws snapped shut where it thought I should be; but instead of finding a feast, it drove itself onto the tip of my knife and, propelled along by its momentum, it slit itself, as Shakespeare would say, from chops to nave. Clouds of brown blood plumed around me. I pushed with my feet and launched myself through the water, away from the sharks. I glanced backwards. The shark I had wounded was thrashing back and forth, and blood was gushing out of its wound into the sea. The other shark had caught the scent and was descending upon its relative.

I pushed myself away from the appalling scene of cannibalism, and sped towards the glittering surface.

My head broke through the water and, with a sense of building triumph, I sucked air into my grateful lungs. For a few moments, I could breathe.

"Thank God!" I gasped.

But then I heard a loud crack—gunfire—and I realized that Gusta and the Mexican Coast Guard were still locked in combat. My fight with the sharks had probably taken less than two minutes. Groaning with weariness, I spun myself round, looking for the boats.

There they were. Gusta's ship had almost disappeared—it wasn't much more than a dot and a cloud of smoky steam. The Mexican ship was much slower, and it was still fairly close to me. I could see the white water kicked up by its screw. But one of its crew, glancing sternwards, caught sight of me and yelled out. Immediately, sailors began to man the stern gun, cranking it around towards me.

I turned landwards. Ahead of me was dry land, the beach and forest. But between it and me was a wide bar of white sand. Right now, safety lay beyond the sand-bar for me. I kicked with my heels, cupped my hands, and swam with all my might for the sand-bar. In a few moments, I had closed the distance. My toes brushed sand, and I dragged myself to my feet, staggering up onto the sand-bar. My heart was pounding in my chest as I turned and stared out across the sea.

The gun in the stern thundered. Rationally, I knew that it was highly unlikely they could hit a single man with a deck gun, but I wasn't thinking rationally, so I threw myself into the sea beyond the sand-bar. It was very shallow water, and didn't even cover me. I heard the frantic whistling of the shell overhead, and a terrific explosion broke out ahead. Sand and fish were thrown out in all directions.

That had been closer than I expected. I scrambled through the shallows, splashing frantically until I reached deeper water. Then I leaped forward into the water, cleaving through the cool blueness. For a moment, I sailed through a weird world, the sun-sparkled surface inches over my head, the white sand inches below it; it was like swimming through an envelope. To my alarm, I saw something silver drift past my eyes, trailing bubbles—a bullet.

Don't panic, I thought: keep calm. Just a few more yards.

But the envelope through which I swam was getting narrower, and I couldn't swim any further.

I wrenched myself to my feet and picked up my feet to dash for the forest. They seemed heavy, because they dragged up water with them, and I ran amidst a torrent of seawater. Behind me came a crackling of gunfire. I glanced back, as I saw that the Coast Guard had taken out a dinghy, and were rowing madly towards me. One seaman stood in the prow, clutching a pistol. Another stood beside him, a rifle tucked into his shoulder. But the motion of the waves made aiming impossible for the moment. I had until they reached the sand-bar; then they would be on solid ground and could take proper aim.

I was out of the water now, and dashed across the hard, dark sand of the margin and onto the hot, soft stuff beyond the tideline. It was so bright in the Caribbean sun that it almost hurt my eyes. And it was difficult to run on. I stumbled a couple of times, sand pluming about me.

Behind me, the dinghy's prow bumped on the sand-bar. The Coast Guard men piled out. Two of them started dragging the dinghy across the sand-bar, while the other two took a few pot-shots at me. I zig-zagged. I didn't have time for any formal prayer; all I could do was scream out, "He-e-elp!" I stumbled on, expecting at any moment to feel the dull pain of a bullet in my back. Another gunshot rang out, and the bullet kicked up a little cloud of sand off to my right.

I ran left.

At the edge of the beach, just before the deep green of the forest, stood a series of low dunes, like a wall. I ran for the dunes and threw myself at them. Another gunshot, followed by a *fsst!* as the bullet smacked into the dune an inch from my shoulder. I scrambled up the dune and rolled to the far side, into a waterlogged ditch behind.

I was safe, for the moment.

I took a quick look around to appraise my situation. A peek over the dunes revealed that the Coast Guard were in the dinghy again, and had almost reached the shore. Behind the dunes was an open expanse, covered by green foliage—hardly any cover there, until I reached the forest of palms behind it.

But that was the way to safety, and now was the time, before the Coast Guard were on the beach.

I picked myself up and ran for it. The foliage through which I dashed was thorny, and snatched at my trousers as I waded through it. In a lot of ways, it was harder going than the shallows.

A voice came from behind me, raised above the rolling of the waves. I couldn't understand much, except the words *señor pirata*. I suppose they were urging me to turn myself in. On the contrary, I reckoned, it was a good idea to run.

They opened fire again. But now they were too late. I pressed myself through a gap between two head-high trees and in among the green light of the jungle. I hurled myself behind the slender bole of a palm tree and paused a moment.

The green closed in about me, stripes and dots of darkness against brilliant sunshine, and the deafening sound of insects and tree frogs. I had thought it would be cooler in here, but I was wrong: the heat seemed to be captured beneath the green canopy, and it pressed me like a vice-grip. All my senses seemed oppressed by the jungle. It seemed like a good idea to give up, to just sink down into the green and sleep.

I forced myself to remain on my feet, and dragged my head around to look at the beach.

I couldn't see much. The dunes obstructed a clear view. But I could see that the customs men were still there, advancing cautiously across the beach, their pistols and rifles held at the ready. They wore tropical whites, darkened in patches by seawater. They would be at the dunes in a few moments, I saw.

I had time. I could rest. In a kind of stupor, I watched the customs men climb to the top of the dunes and scan the forest, their hands shielding their eyes.

They consulted with one another, but evidently concluded that they would never be able to find me in the jungle. So they turned about and returned to their dinghy. After a few minutes of rowing, they reached the customs boat. A blast of smoke went up from its funnel, and it turned about and steamed away.

I guessed that Gusta had got away; if they had sunk the *Fortuna*, there would be a lot of debris floating on the waves. And they had evidently not captured her.

I sank back against the palm tree and breathed a sigh of relief. I didn't move. My body ached from head to foot, and my clothes were rent all over.

Something disturbed the palm-fronds above my head, and I saw the scarlet wing of a parrot as it glided from one tree to another.

All I had to do now, I reflected, was get to Campeche.

All? I had no idea where I was, in a country I'd never visited, whose language I didn't speak. I knew Gusta's brother had a parish nearby, but I didn't know how to get there.

I began to wonder why on earth I'd agreed to finish my trip with him.

I wasn't nearly rested enough, and felt that it would be glorious to stay there a long while, and perhaps even sleep. But I forced myself onto my feet. I started walking, keeping the beach in view on my right. If I continued this way, I reasoned, I should be walking north, and I would find Fr. Sarín's parish.

I hoped I didn't have far to walk—I was keenly aware of looking like a waterlogged scarecrow, my clothes torn and streaked with sand and salt, my hair tousled. But I hadn't gone far when I came across a narrow river, which I followed to a lake of still water, with a church standing on the far bank. It was white-walled with terracotta roof tiles and a bell-tower of bare stone. The walls of the cemetery were

63

bare stone too, and at one corner a tall mausoleum rose to a Gothic point. Weary to the bone, I stumbled through the lych-gate and along the path to the door. Dragging it open, I dipped my fingers in the holy water, made the Sign of the Cross, and entered. The interior was airy and clean, the walls whitewashed, the windows unglazed so that a breeze wafted in delightfully from outside. So did birds, flittering about over my head, twittering to one another as I walked down the aisle. Everything in the church, I saw, was spartan, but the reredos was magnificent. It was intricately carved and overlaid with gold leaf. It framed two ranks of saints' pictures, all turned to look at the Blessed Virgin and St. Joseph. The Sacred Heart stood directly over the crucifix.

I genuflected with a weary knee, and knelt for a prayer of thanks. At length, I sat down.

Moments later, I was asleep.

CHAPTER 6
WELCOME TO MEXICO

I woke up some time later—I could tell, because the length of the shadows was different—to find a priest, with a seamed, brown face and a bushy white moustache, bending over me, his eyes brimming with concern.

"*Estás bien, hijo mío?*" he asked.

I had no idea what he was trying to say, though he said it several more times before I broke in with, "Sorry, Padre, *no habla español.*"

He giggled at this, and said, "*No, Yo puedo hablar en español—tu no se puede hablar español.*" And he laughed again.

"I don't understand," I said miserably. "Do you speak English? *Hablas* English?"

"No, no, no," said the priest, still laughing mercilessly at me. "*No hablo Inglés. Solo hablo español y latín.*"

"Latin?" I said. He nodded. I thought hard. I knew no Spanish, and all I knew of Latin was the Mass. Maybe I could piece together something from that. How many years had I heard Mass in Latin? I ought to know something. "*Pater,*" I said slowly, "*non sum dignus sub tectum meum.*" The priest covered his mouth to conceal a snigger. I tried to ignore

65

the gesture. What else was there? I jabbed my thumbs at my clothing. "*Munda vestris meis,*" I said, hoping I was getting the alterations right. The priest cackled with laughter. He laughed so hard that he had to sit down and wipe his eyes.

"*Me haces reir, Inglés!*" he said. Then he translated into Latin: "*Ridiculus es, Angle.*" Both phrases were equally obscure to me. "*Quid faciam tibi?*" asked the priest. He tried to mime his words: he shrugged, pointed to himself, and then to me. I thought I understood. He was asking me what I wanted.

"Er . . . *panem? Vinum? Aquam?*" I said hesitantly. "*Et homo qui dicet English?*"

"Ah!" The priest rose from the pew and beckoned for me to follow him. We genuflected before the tabernacle, walked along the aisle, and exited. He led me through the cemetery and into a rectory just outside the wall. Inside, the priest showed me into a tiny kitchen with a wood stove and a sink with a pump. Reaching into a pantry, he brought out some bread, cheese, and an orange. He poured some water from a pitcher into a glass for me.

"*Accipe,*" he said, "*et manduca!*" He roared with laughter again, and added, "*Vado,*" (miming walking) "*ad oppidum*" (and he pointed out of the window at a collection of houses that lay a few hundred yards down the road) "*et arcessendum homo*" (he mimed beckoning someone to come with him) "*qui loquitur*" (he mimed speaking by opening and shutting his hand rapidly) "*Anglorum.*" And in a mock English accent he said, "Give me some roast beef!" and roared with laughter again. Then, collecting a hat from beside the door, he strode off down the road, his cassock flapping as he went.

I prayed a speedy Grace and entertained myself with the food while he was gone, and it tasted like ambrosia to one who had eaten nothing all day. The time thus passed swiftly until the priest returned with a man in his early twenties. He wore a waistcoat and tie over a white shirt, a wide-brimmed hat, and gaiters. He was dark-complexioned, with a long moustache. Entering the house, he said, "*Hola, señor.* I am Juan Mendez. I learn English at the Pontifical University in Mexico City. Fr. Sarín tells me you need help."

"Fr. Sarín?" I repeated. "Does he have a brother called Gusta?"

Juan and the priest conversed in Spanish for a few moments then, grinning, Juan turned back to me. "*Si, señor,* he has a brother called Augusto, or Gusta. He says that if you know Gusta, tell him his brother would like to talk with him. It has been a very long time since he last went to confession."

I grinned too. "If I see him again, I'll tell him." Another exchange in Spanish followed. In the end, I had to break in. "Can you help me get to Campeche?" I asked.

"Campeche?" repeated Juan. "It is possible, I think. But it is very far, *señor*, over forty miles. It would take two days to get there. Fr. Sarín goes to Campeche every month, to see the bishop." He and Fr. Sarín spoke rapidly to one another for a few moments. Then Juan said, "He is not going to Campeche for another week. Could you wait that long, *señor*?"

I shook my head. "I'm afraid I have urgent business there. Is there somewhere close I can send a telegram?" I wondered.

"*Si, señor*—we have a post office. I will take you there. You have money?"

"Not a penny," I lamented.

Juan said something to Fr. Sarín, who disappeared and returned a moment later with a few copper coins. Grinning, he said, "*Reddite quae Caesaris sunt Caesari!*" He laughed again, and Juan joined in. As I dropped the coins into my pocket, Fr. Sarín handed me a stack of clothes he evidently thought would fit me—all black, of course.

As we were leaving, I shook the priest's hand. "*Dominus vobiscum*," I said.

"*Et cum spiritu tuo*," he replied. Then, making the Sign of the Cross solemnly, he spoke a few words of blessing, and Juan led me off to the village—a dirt road with shacks on either side, their roofs mostly thatched. Palm trees hung their fronds over the roofs. Juan led me to the most modern-looking building in the village, which looked as if it had been built about a hundred years ago. Inside, he negotiated with the elderly man behind the counter, who eventually took my money and painstakingly tapped out my message in English.

"You must excuse Pedro," said Juan. "He does not know English so well." He grinned and shook my hand. "Let me know if there is anything else I can help you with, *señor*," he concluded, and left me.

I waited about half an hour in the dark interior of the post office until Wilmer's reply arrived: MESSAGE RECEIVED STOP WILL PICK UP STOP ESTIMATE TWO HOURS STOP. I stuffed the reply into my pocket and wandered out into the street and back to the church to wait for Wilmer.

I don't know how long Wilmer actually took to find me, because seawater had leaked into my watch and spoiled the clockwork. But I noticed that the sunlight slanted through the windows of the church closer to the horizontal than to the vertical when the doors behind me opened, and Wilmer sauntered in, his hands in his pockets.

"Why, there you are, old sport!" he cried.

I held a finger to my lips. "Have a little reverence," I scolded him.

"Sorry," returned Wilmer, in a whisper. "Are you a fish-eater, then?" I sighed and nodded. "Sorry again," said Wilmer. I got up from the pew, genuflected, and walked outside with him. He had brought a Model-T Ford, about ten years old, which had been converted into a truck. Wilmer cranked the engine a few times, climbed in behind the steering wheel, and threw her into gear.

"So, what happened?" asked Wilmer. I told him briefly of my adventures after leaving the *Esperanza*—omitting, of course, Gusta's reservations about him and Lychfield. At my conclusion, he gave a long whistle, mopping his brow with a handkerchief. "That was an original idea," he said, "finishing your trip with a pirate. Glad you made it, though."

I rested my elbow on the open window and gazed out at the dirt road. We passed a few pedestrians returning from a market. They rode bicycles or tricycles or, more often, led donkeys, burdened with a few unsold goods.

"Well, anyway," Wilmer went on, "I've hired bearers for the trip to Xulamqamtun. As soon as Ariadne gets here, we can set out—it'll probably be a three-day hike." He mopped his brow again. "Nasty jungle," he commented. "At least the Professor has installed air conditioning throughout Xulamqamtun."

"Air conditioning?" I inquired, my curiosity piqued.

Wilmer glanced sideways at me. "It's a way of cooling and de-humidifying air. It's been around for a while."

"Interesting," I remarked. "How does it work?"

Wilmer shrugged. "How would I know?" he said. "I turn a knob and cool air comes out of a box."

The drive lasted a little under two hours. Night was falling when we reached Campeche, and I was able to bathe and climb into bed between clean, cool sheets.

Two days later, on Saturday, my luggage arrived at the hotel. It was carried up to my room by the only bell-boy who spoke any English at all. He told me that it he didn't know who had delivered it. It came with a note of apology that carried the faintest whiff of cigar-smoke.

Almost a week passed, Wilmer chaffing at the delay, before Ari's steamship arrived. She was a lovely old girl, single-funneled, with huge paddles on the sides like an American riverboat.

"Did you sail that all the way from New York?" I asked.

"We changed in Havana," replied Ari. "American steamers sailing to Mexico are few, owing to the Revolution."

"She's a beauty," I commented, as I helped Fritz load up a horse-drawn cab with their luggage.

We chatted about the voyage all the way to the hotel. In the lobby, I spoke briefly with the concierge about getting a couple of drinks delivered, then we went up to the room. The drinks were ready a couple of minutes after we had arrived.

"Right." Ari stood, her arms akimbo, framed by the window of our hotel room so that early afternoon sun outlined her gently. Fritz was moving back and forth in the background, unpacking Ari's things and tidying up some of the things I'd meant to put away later. "What do you want to know about your friend Professor Lychfield?"

I handed her a gin and tonic and dropped into a wicker chair under the cool of the ceiling fan. There was something truculent in her manner, something that made me uneasy. "I haven't seen him in some years," I mused. "Has he greyed much since then?"

Ari didn't speak for a moment. "You're being facetious," she observed. "What do you want to know that's important?"

"Hey, Fritz," I said, noting something he was handling lovingly, "is that a Mauser?"

"*Jawohl*, Herr McCracken," said Fritz eagerly, handing it to me—it looked like a large holster, except that it was carved from wood, with a catch and hinges at the wide end. I flipped it open and from inside slid out a hand-gun. It was an old reliable model, the Mauser C96, top-loaded with a stripper clip, the distinctive shape of the magazine bulging in front of the trigger. The wooden container was actually a stock, into which you could slot the hilt of the Mauser, converting it into something like a rifle. "The Luger Herr Tesla gave me," Fritz explained, "she jammed. This in the Luger is a design flaw.

The Mauser I bought from a nice man in New York just before we sailed." Fritz grinned lopsidedly. "Frau McCracken also made some purchases there."

"I bet she did," I commented, slotting the hilt into the stock and then taking it apart again. The hilt of the gun itself was emblazoned with a red 9, indicating the number of shots it could fire. "The Mauser's lovely," I concluded.

"Have you quite finished?" demanded Ari. I handed the Mauser back to Fritz and turned my attention to her. I felt a little guilty at ignoring her like that, but I really didn't want to hear the nasty things she would have to say about Professor Lychfield. "According to a friend of mine, who has a friend at Imperial, Wilmer's not being quite straight about Lychfield's reasons for leaving."

"Really?"

"Yes, really," replied Ari. I took a sip from my gin and tonic—very refreshing on a hot afternoon like this. "If Lychfield left because he received a grant, nobody at Imperial knew about it."

"Lychfield didn't get on well with the other professors," I explained. "You have to remember, he's a genius, but in a very narrow field. The other professors didn't have any respect for his studies."

"Mining?" I nodded. A crease appeared between Ari's beautifully arched eyebrows. "The Royal School of Mining has been a part of Imperial for years. How could it be more respected than that?"

"He didn't teach in the School of Mining, though," I said.

"Why not, if he was an expert in it?" Ari demanded. I didn't have an answer—I was surprised by these things. I'd known them, of course, but somehow I hadn't pieced together all the facts in quite the way Ari did.

"His degree isn't in mining," I told Ari. "I suppose he's really just an amateur, even if he's very gifted. Professors tend to dislike gifted amateurs—like the Scotland Yard men and Sherlock Holmes."

"How do you know the other professors disliked him?" inquired Ari. "Did you see anything to make you think that?"

"Yes, of course I did," I said at once; then, after a short pause, I said, "Well, actually, no, I didn't actually see anything like that, not actually *see*."

"Quite." Ari pressed her lips together triumphantly. "They weren't hostile," she added. "It was just Lychfield's paranoia."

"Wait a moment," I objected, sitting bolt upright, "you can't accuse Professor Lychfield of . . . what's paranoia?"

"A mental state characterized by delusions," Ari explained. "According to Rolf, my friend, Lychfield had made a pest of himself—he was very insistent about certain pedagogical matters."

"Peda-what?" I asked. "Is that something to do with feet?" Ari frowned. "Or children?" I added hopefully.

"Teaching!" she chided me. "Pedagogy—teaching. Don't you know any words over two syllables?" I opened my mouth to mention a *piston-rod*, but I couldn't remember whether it was a three-syllable word or two hyphenated words. "For your information," Ari went on, quite angry by now, "in simple words, he refused to let go of some weird ideas he had. The Rector was going to issue a severe reprimand, but somehow Lychfield heard about it and turned in his resignation."

There was a long silence. Through the open window, I could faintly hear the street sounds. The curtain stirred in a listless breeze. I said, "You haven't touched your gin and tonic. It's very good, especially on a hot day."

Ari looked at her gin and tonic, but didn't drink any. "Don't you think that's a bit suspicious?"

I shrugged. "Not really," I said. "I think I'd leave rather than let the Rector reprimand me."

"Would you?" Ari's expression had darkened somewhat. "And leave your wife and children without support?"

"I don't have any children," I said blithely.

For a moment, an indescribable expression descended on Ari's face. For a split second, her eyes narrowed. Her lips pursed slightly. Her jaw moved left and right almost imperceptibly. But it was all over in less than a second. "Lychfield does," she said. "A boy. And that's another thing—why aren't his wife and son with him at Xulamqamtun?"

"I don't know," I said, a little irritably. All this excessive attention to detail was beginning to make me a bit impatient. "As I remember, they were a little sensitive to climate—they wouldn't have cared at all for Mexico." I loosened my collar a little. "I don't care much for this heat myself. Anyway, Lychfield's boy must be almost ready to go to university himself now."

"He's in his last year at LAMDA," Ari informed me.

"At what?"

"The London Academy of Music and Dramatic Art," she explained. "He's studying to become an actor."

"Acting?" I said. "That's a bit of a departure. Lychfield always wanted him to study engineering." I got to my feet and, taking her chin gently in my hands, kissed her lightly on the lips. I said, "Sweetheart, I've known Lychfield for years. He's one of the most dependable blokes I know."

"Well, he *was* dependable . . . what, ten years ago? Fifteen?"

"I can't see that he would have changed that much. Look, if Lychfield isn't doing what he's supposed to be doing, I'll just have a word with him—

he'll listen to me. Everything will be fine. Don't worry, all right?"

"Don't worry!" Ari exploded all of a sudden. She pulled away from me and slammed her drink down on a table so hard that about a third of it spilled over the mahogany. "Why are you covering for him? This adventure is very risky. We need to assess the dangers coolly."

"I'm not covering for him," I objected, a little chastened at what seemed her sudden anger. "But I don't see why it's so important—it's just another jaunt, like Rio, or Thera, or Zun, or the Yukon."

Ari looked up at me, her bottom lip quivering, her eyes brimming with tears. I was struck by her sudden change in emotion, and a little frightened. "But it's not just us this time," she said. "I told you I had a doctor's appointment back in New York. Well, guess what? There's going to be someone extra on this 'little jaunt.'"

I was confused. "Well, we always take Fritz with us," I said.

"Of course we'll take Fritz. But there'll be someone else on this trip." She paused, apparently expecting a reaction from me. But I was confused and remained silent. She explained patiently, "We're expecting a baby."

"A baby?"

Suddenly, all of the silence outside seemed to flood in through the open window and fill the hotel room. It swirled noiselessly about the floor, crept inaudibly up the legs of the bed, then washed soundlessly across the table-top, almost carrying away my gin and tonic.

"We're going to have a baby?" I said, still struggling with the concept. Ari nodded. "Great Scott!" I exclaimed. "This is wonderful—I can teach him to build little bridges and steam engines, and . . ."

"Mac," interrupted Ari, "that might not be entirely appropriate."

"You think he might not want to build bridges and steam engines?"

"No, but *he* might be a *she*."

"And why wouldn't *she* be interested in bridges and steam engines?" I retorted. "What a thing to suggest about my daughter! Oh, wait a minute!" I took the gin and tonic from the table she'd set it on. "You shouldn't be drinking this," I chided her.

"I haven't touched it."

"Good." I drained it in a single gulp. "Sit down, and have a rest." I pushed her into a seat. "Are you warm enough?"

"Mac, we're in Mexico in the summertime—I'm quite warm enough. I'm well enough to handle a little adventure. But I'd like to know that you're taking the risks seriously enough, that your head isn't swayed by this old professor of yours."

"Well, of course it isn't," I said. I collapsed into my own chair. "Look, if something isn't right when

we get there, we'll just come right back. I promise."
An idea suddenly occurred to me. "And we can have
Fr. Sarín bless us, and the baby, if you like."

"Who is Fr. Sarín?" Ari asked. I described my
adventures with Gusta and the Coast Guard. "Well,"
she said in the end, "if you're perfectly sure, then I
won't worry."

CHAPTER 7
INTO THE JUNGLE

I take it back," Ari said, ten hours later. "I'm worried now."

She, Fritz and I had driven the truck with the supplies out to the edge of town, where Wilmer had told us to meet him with the bearers he had hired. The sun had barely risen, and it cast long blue shadows across the road. Already, it was a hot day, and the jungle was cacophonous with millions of tiny buzzing creatures. We stood beside an old stone bridge, and two boats were moored in the shadow of its single arch.

Wilmer had lined the bearers up along the side of the road. There were eight of them in all. They were all between about sixteen and twenty-two years old. And they were all girls, with long, dark hair and sultry brown eyes. Each one of them was stunningly beautiful.

I had to stifle a laugh. "Wilmer," I said, "you've never equipped an expedition before, have you?"

"What do you mean?" demanded Wilmer. He was fanning himself with a slouch hat, and had exchanged his white suit for khaki shirt and jodhpurs, knee-length brown boots and a canvas vest with lots of pockets.

"Well," I said, making a hopeless gesture towards the bearers, "they're all girls."

He cast a glance across them. "Yes, they are," he said, as if noticing for the first time. "Well, I looked at a lot of natives for this trip, and I guarantee, these were the very best." He gave them some instructions in Spanish, and the girls began unloading the truck and carrying the packages down a narrow path to the boats.

"The very best at what?" asked Ari.

"Oh, carrying things," replied Wilmer, with the air of one who doesn't have time for such bothersome details, "guiding us along the river, that sort of thing." He turned to Ari with a puzzled expression on his face. "Would you like me to ask them to go home?" he asked. "I can do that, but I've always believed women can do most of the things only men do nowadays, Ariadne."

"There's no need for that," replied Ari. "And you can call me Mrs. McCracken."

"Really? But I thought—all right, then," said Wilmer, a little confused.

"What will they do when we get to Hop-from-a-pontoon?" I asked.

"Xulamqamtun," Ari corrected me *sotto voce*.

"They'll be working for me—running errands, cleaning my shirts and so forth—you wouldn't believe how many shirts you can go through in this climate. It's blessed hot."

I nodded. "The jungle often is," I remarked. With a sigh, I gave a nod. "Well, it's probably too late to find other bearers now. Let's get moving."

I picked up one of the last crates from the back of the truck, hefted it onto my shoulder, and carried it down to the waiting boats. The girls had almost finished loading the rest of the supplies, and they had done quite a good job of it—I only had to shift one crate to redistribute the weight. When I'd finished, the gunwales were all of an equal distance from the brown mirror of the water. I sat myself in the stern, next to the outboard motor. Ari boarded, the little boat bobbing slightly as she did so. She lowered herself into the prow and made the Sign of the Cross.

"I didn't know you were afraid of boats," I said.

"I'm not," she replied. In a low voice, she added, "It's this expedition that scares me."

"I thought you were all right after talking to Fr. Sarín," I protested.

"Fr. Sarín is a delightful gentleman," she replied, "but Wilmer is a creep."

"Let's just keep our eyes open," I counseled, "and be ready to make a move if necessary. I'm sure Lychfield is on the level, but if he's not, we'll be gone quicker than you can say *J. W. Howlett's patent adjustable frictional gearing*."

The boat bobbed again, and we both looked up to see Fritz picking his way gingerly through the supplies towards the stern of the boat. He cradled the Mauser in his arms like a baby. Above us, we heard the truck's engine cough and splutter and then settle into a single throbbing note. It idled for a few moments, then the driver shifted gear. We listened to the sound of the engine dwindling for a while.

Then, casually at first, but inexorably, the sound of the jungle took over, uninterrupted, uniform, monotonous. It was like a blanket of sound that had been laid over our conversation and, one by one, each of us ceased talking. Manuel, our guide, called out from the other boat. I pulled on the starter while Ari cast off. We slid into the middle of the river.

Puttering into the tangled green of the jungle was like entering something profoundly alien, but at the same time familiar, like a half-remembered memory from early childhood. Dark, living curtains of vines hung between us and the jungle's shadowy secrets, with gnarled trunks peeping out like the knees of wizened old men. Cedars, mahoganies and sapodillas towered over the brambles. From time to time, we caught sight of the dark rosette of a brome-liad.

"Ceiba trees," said Ari, pointing. They stood over the mess of the jungle, a spreading canopy over a silvery, bottle-shaped bole. "They were sacred to the Mayans—according to their mythology, a ceiba tree grew through the centre of the universe, like Yggdrasil in Norse mythology."

"Good for keeping an eye on things," I observed, noting how they seemed mostly to grow at bends in the river. "Useful for spotting enemies."

Our journey continued most of the day, with me at the tiller, Manuel shouting back directions that Ari occasionally translated for me. In the early afternoon, the clouds gathered and a light drizzle fell for about an hour. Afterwards, the sun came out, and the humidity seemed to wrap about us like a damp sleeping bag.

After a few more hours, Manuel turned his tiller, pointing the nose of the boat towards the left bank. He cut the motor. I followed suit, and instantly the noise of the jungle grew all about us. The buzz of insects and tree frogs, the cries of monkeys and the squawks of birds combined in a kind of strange symphony, though we could see none of the musicians. The constant breeze of the journey slowed, and the heat pressed in all around us.

Our boat slid up onto the shore. The rain had transformed our landing place into a plain of black mud, into which we all sank an inch as we stepped ashore to sort our gear. I lifted Ari out of the boat and set her down beyond the mud.

"You don't feel like two people," I observed in a whisper.

"Not yet," agreed Ari.

I glanced up at the angle of the sunlight through the trees. "We've got about three hours of daylight left," I said. "We can get quite a long way in that time."

Wilmer looked up from where he was directing the girls on bringing the crates out of the boat. "Or we could camp here," he suggested. "Not much point going on now, old sport."

"What do you think, Manuel?"

Manuel shrugged. "You are the *gringos locos*," he said. "You tell me."

We ended up camping for the night, which I found very frustrating, as we could have traveled another six or eight miles in the daylight that remained to us. The consolation was that Fritz made *panuchos*—flour tortillas stuffed with black beans and onions, and topped with chicken.

"What's that green stuff?" I asked, picking up a jar and sniffing it; the spices and pepper teased my nostrils and made my stomach rumble.

"It is called *xnipec*, Herr McCracken," replied Fritz, stirring it carefully. "I prepare it before we come away—some Mexican peppers, spring onions, garlic, and orange juice."

"Orange juice?" Ari said in disbelief. She dipped a fingertip in it and tasted it, making a yummy noise as she did so. "Does it go on the *panuchos*?"

"*Jawohl*," replied Fritz, turning the chicken in the frying pan. It was covered with a reddish blend of spices, and beginning to blacken in places. "And now, please and *danke*, Herr McCracken, Frau McCracken—do not the artist crowd, please."

By the time he was finished, he had attracted the attention of the bearers, who crowded about him, cooing and making approving noises at the deft way he flipped the tortilla back and forth so that it browned without blackening. When he topped the *panuchos* with chicken, lettuce and tomato, and drizzled the *xnipec* over it, they cried out delightedly, "*Que lindo!*" In the end, he had to make enough *panuchos* for everyone. Wilmer, bereft of his bevy of bearers, slouched over to our fire and sat down. Fritz triumphantly dropped a *panucho* onto a pewter plate for him and he began to eat it sulkily, without even a *thank you.*

The *panuchos* were a culinary miracle—the solid background of the black beans and onions complimented by the fireworks of the spicy chicken and the tangy *xnipec*.

But more wonderful, in a lot of ways, was seeing short, odd-looking Fritz surrounded by an admiring crowd of Mexican beauties.

"I think Fritz might have found himself a sweetheart in Mexico," I mused to Ari.

"Hardly," she replied. "He's married already."

I almost choked on my *panucho*. "Married?"

"Yes, to a lady called Helga. They weren't able to get out of Germany before the War began."

"He has children as well?"

"Fourteen. Eight girls and six boys. Two sets of twins among the girls."

"Fourteen!" I wiped my brow. "That's a heck of a number to beat." I frowned. "How do you know that and I don't?"

Ari leaned over and kissed me on the nose. "I probably listen a bit more than you do," she said.

"Fritz!" I said, when he settled down beside us to eat his own supper. "Mrs. McCracken tells me you have fourteen children back in Germany. Fourteen!"

"Some of them came in twos, Herr McCracken," replied Fritz apologetically.

"Do you ever hear from them?"

"Not in almost a year," replied Fritz. "The War—it happened so quickly, I could not arrange for Helga and my little ones to get out of Germany in time."

"I'm sorry."

"Perhaps soon the War will be over," suggested Fritz. "Then we will all be together again—in England, perhaps."

"Or Scotland," I countered. "That would be better."

We retired for the night shortly afterwards, and drifted off to sleep with the cacophonous night noises all around us.

But we were awoken in the small hours of the morning when the tent flap was roughly yanked aside. I opened my eyes blearily, and the blurry image slowly coalesced.

Staring into my tent was a tattooed face, dark of complexion and fierce of aspect.

Ari and I sat bolt upright in amazement. The fierce face scowled at us for a moment, and then its owner gestured for us to leave the tent.

Ari and I pulled on clothes quickly and left the tent to join the bearers, Fritz, Manuel and Wilmer outside. Wilmer wore pajamas. We were surrounded by an odd collection of figures, eerily lit by the moonlight. They wore little except loincloths, elaborate armbands shaped like snakes, and wide necklaces. Some wore tall, feathered helmets; others wore long hair, tied back from their faces. All were tattooed on their arms, stomachs, and faces. One of them, who appeared from his more ostentatious dress to be their leader, had tiny human heads suspended from a belt.

"Who are they, Manuel?" I asked. "What do they want?"

"They are the Ququmatz, *señor*," answered Manuel in a hoarse whisper. "I think they want our heads."

CHAPTER 8
THE LOST CITY

The chief of the Ququmatz strode impressively up to us, his eyes wide and glaring, his nostrils flared, the corners of his mouth turned grimly downwards. He came to a halt in front of the girls. Instantly, one of the girls wailed in terror, the others joining in a second later. The chief ran his eyes up and down each one in turn. He aimed a comment over his shoulder and his warriors all laughed and pointed at the girls with their fingers or weapons.

Next, the chief inspected Ari. She returned his stare, one eyebrow raised quizzically. The chief laughed, and passed on to me. He spent less time examining me, then Fritz, then Manuel, in silence. Finally, he came to Wilmer. Wilmer shook in his pajamas, and his face, drained of all colour, was turned towards the earth. The chief reached out, took his chin, rather roughly, and forced him to look up.

Seeing Wilmer's face, the chief's eyes sprang wide, and he took a step backwards. He spoke to his warriors, two of whom came forwards and stood on either side of him, subjecting Wilmer to an intense scrutiny. Their weapons glinted in the light from the campfire.

Wilmer fell to his knees, his hands clasped before him. "Please don't kill me!" he wailed.

Three faces leaned in close to Wilmer's. They had cheekbones that could have cut steel, and their noses were great arcs springing from a place just above their eyebrows. The chief reached out with one hand, powerful and sinewy. Wilmer flinched, and I felt a growing shame for him. What was the point of making a life out of jungle adventure if the local tribes scared you so much? So much better to stay in the suburban bungalows.

But the chief didn't harm Wilmer; he merely pinched some of the silk of his pajamas, rubbed it between his fingers, and laughed.

"Wheel-moor?" he said in halting syllables.

Wilmer caught his breath. Ari and I cried out in surprise. Wilmer stammered, "Y-y-yes, sir, that's m-m-me—I'm Wi-Wilmer."

The chief pointed to himself. "Ajawchakka," he said. Then, seeing that this was not in itself an adequate explanation, he repeated with emphasis, "*Ajawchakka!*"

"Ajawchakka?" said Wilmer, in a daze.

"I think that's his name," Ari suggested. "He's introducing himself."

"*U Ququmatz kinich,*" said the chief, pointing to himself again. "*Bix a bei, Wheel-moor? Bix a bei?*"

Wilmer stared dumbly at him. Turning to Ari, he asked, "Do you know what he's saying, Ar—Mrs. McCracken?"

"I don't know for certain," Ari told Wilmer. "Perhaps he's saying, 'How do you do.'"

"How do I say, 'I'm doing fine?'"

She frowned, her face a study of concentration. "*Bix a bei*—how . . . do-you . . . do. *Bix—how. Bei—do* or *doing*. There was a word for 'okay.' Rolf told me what it was. What was it? *Malob*! That's it—try *Bei malob*."

Wilmer swallowed, his Adam's apple jumping up and down, and he said, "*B-b-bei malob. Bei malob*, all right?"

The chief's eyes opened wide. "*Bei malob!*" he exclaimed. "*Cu thanoob 'Bei malob!'*"

"What's he saying?" I asked.

"I think he's just repeating Wilmer—he's surprised he knew what to say. *Cu*—he, she, or it; *thanoob*—said. Okay, I'm getting the hang of it."

"How does he know me?" Wilmer wondered.

Ari and I shook our heads. The chief turned back to Wilmer. "*Yan ua a bin ti Xulamqamtun?*" he asked.

"Yes!" cried Wilmer, nodding vigorously at hearing a familiar word.

"*Yan ua a bin ti Pro-hess-sorr Leech-hilt?*" inquired the chief.

"Yes! Yes! Yes!" said Wilmer with enthusiasm.

"I don't know why he's so enthusiastic," said Ari out of the corner of her mouth. "For all he knows, he's telling him he's eaten Professor Lychfield."

"Can you tell what he's really saying?" I asked, praying he hadn't eaten Lychfield.

"*Yan ua a bin ti*—that's how he began both those questions," Ari explained. "So he sees a connection between Xulamqamtun and Professor Lychfield, naturally enough, since Lychfield is *at* Xulamqamtun. So *yan ua a bin ti* probably means 'Are you going to?' But I don't know which word means 'what' yet."

"*Ma bin ti Xulamqamtun,*" said the chief, very loudly and very slowly into Wilmer's face, as if he were explaining something to a slow-witted child. He mimed walking with his fingers, pointed to himself and his warriors, then thrust his forefinger towards the jungle. Then he pointed to each of us in turn. "*Talaa,*" he finished.

"Okay, I get it," said Ari. "*Bin ti* means 'going to,' and I'm guessing *yan* is a word indicating that the sentence is a question—they usually come at the beginning of sentences. That means *ua* means 'you' and *ma* probably means 'we.' He said, 'We're going to Xulamqamtun.' And I can remember a little of the conjunctions from Suarez' *Pre-Colombian Languages.*" Stepping forward, she said to the chief, "*Ma*

92

yetel ua bin ti Xulamqamtun." She bowed her head in thanks.

The chief turned to Ari in amazement. To his warriors, he said, "*Hach x-cichpam le x-chupalo.*" They nodded in vigorous agreement, waved their weapons, shouted and made animal noises.

"What did he say?" I asked, stepping a little closer to Ari. "That response didn't look good."

Ari blushed. "I think he said I was the prettiest of all these girls," she told me. "The light's pretty bad."

"I get it!" cried Wilmer all of a sudden. We all turned towards him. "I get it—how they know me. These are the natives that help us out at Xulamqamtun."

"Then why didn't you recognize them right away?" I asked.

"Well, they look different in this light," said Wilmer faintly.

"You mean you never looked at them closely enough," said Ari, wrinkling her nose. Looking back at the warriors, she said, "I think they want to help us get to Xulamqamtun."

"*Talaa,*" said the chief, beckoning to us.

Ari stepped towards him, spoke a few words, and pointed at the tents and supplies. After a few exchanges, Ajawchakka understood what Ari was trying to tell him, and barked out a series of commands to his men. They started taking the tents down and collecting the supplies. Ari sauntered back to our group. "The Ququmatz will guide us to Xulamqamtun," she said. "Mayan isn't really very difficult, once you get used to it. Theirs is a little primitive—they've been living in the jungle for centuries, so it doesn't sound like the language spoken in Campeche, for example, or along the coast. But we don't need the girls any more."

"Oh, but can we really do without them?" asked Wilmer. One of the girls brought him a couple of Fritz's enchiladas and he accepted them with a *"Gracias, amiga!"*

"Le x-chupalo tan u bizic le kekeno u yoch!" said Ajawchakka, and all the warriors laughed heartily. Ari joined in.

"What did he say?" asked Wilmer.

Ari shrugged. "He was noting what good servants these girls would make."

"He's right," admitted Wilmer. "I mean, not that I need a servant or anything, but . . . "

"I think perhaps," I said, "that the girls should go back to Campeche. Manuel, would you take them, please?"

"Desde luego!" said Manuel. "Of course, *señor*— I will take the beautiful ladies back to Campeche. But you do not need a guide?"

"It looks like the Ququmatz will be guiding us," I said, "though I'm not wild about being guided through the jungle by a bunch of head-hunters."

"I'm going to get an enchilada," said Ari, moving off towards where Fritz, surrounded by his cooing admirers, was making a hasty breakfast. I fell into step beside her.

"So, what did the chief really say about Wilmer and the girls?" I asked in a low voice.

Ari grinned. "He said, 'Look how that girl takes the pig his food,'" she replied. We laughed for a while, then sat down beside the campfire to enjoy Fritz's magnificent breakfast.

My mouth was still tingling with delight when we said goodbye to the girls and Manuel, who climbed into the boats for their return to Campeche. Shortly afterwards, the Ququmatz shouldered the supplies, Fritz threw water over the fire, and we trekked off through the jungle towards Xula-mqamtun.

We talked a lot at first—mainly, Ari talked to the Ququmatz, busily compiling information about their language in her brain. I didn't feel much like talking to Wilmer, who was a little sulky on account of having to let the girls go. The sun climbed, and our shirts began to stick to our backs. Mosquitos hung in clouds before our faces. We trudged along a muddy track, which occasionally emerged into clearings where the sun shimmered off stagnant pools. If we had to cross one of these clearings, we found that its apparent solidity was largely fictitious, and the mud sucked on our boots, threatening to slurp them off our feet and swallow them for ever.

The next day, the trail changed, and we began to climb dry and stony slopes, the cumbersome weight of the packs cutting into our shoulders. Towards the end of the day, our steps began to crackle on twigs and fallen palm fronds.

It was halfway through the next day's trek that we mounted the summit of a hill, and gazed out across a green valley. Protruding from the dense undergrowth were a pair of grey pyramids. We had come at last to Xulamqamtun.

Beside me, Ari sighed. "*Xulamqamtun u mas hadzutil le x-lac cahobo,*" she said. I cocked an eyebrow in inquiry. "Xulamqamtun is the most beautiful of the ruined cities," she translated. "See what I mean? Quite an easy language, when you get used to it."

"That's easy for you to say," I commented wryly.

But she was right—it was a beautiful sight, this lost city. Innumerable steps led up the side of one pyramid, to a temple that looked like an enormous throne, with arms and a back carved in fantastic designs. It looked as if some barbaric god could take his seat there and survey all of the surrounding jungle as his own. At the top of the other pyramid, light reflected from what seemed to be glass. Between them was an open area, where the grass was cut short and the ground was level. Other buildings, their roofs crumbled so they were open to the sky, stood in the shadow of the two great pyramids. Beyond them, dense and green, the jungle stretched far away in all directions.

"*Talaa*," urged Ajawchakka, beckoning us on down the further slope. A few moments later, the treetops rose around us, and the lost city was lost again for the time being.

We shouldered our way through the bush for most of the afternoon, sometimes descending, sometimes on the level. When we finally reached the city, it came upon us quite suddenly. Vines and brambles stood before us, apparently impenetrable. I hacked left and right with a machete, the vines fell apart, and there it was: Xulamqamtun. To each side stood buildings six or seven stories high. Long shadows lay across the grass, for the sun was beginning to set. Further away, silhouetted against the cobalt of the sky, stood the pyramids, the glass at the top of the smaller of them blazing with golden light.

"Why does the top of the pyramid shine like that?" I asked Wilmer as he drew level with me. "It looks like the sun reflecting on glass."

"It is," replied Wilmer wearily, fanning himself with his hat. "That's Lychfield's house."

We entered the city, walking between the ivy-clad walls. I felt a little like a boy who has played with toy trains all his life, and then sees the real thing—unimaginably huger than anything he had ever imagined, and just a little frightening in its reality. But a steam locomotive is a noisy thing, and these ruins were silent. The masons who had put stone upon stone to build these walls had been long dead a thousand years before the birth of Jesus, and they had left their silence in the stones themselves. Even the jungle creatures seemed to fall back, muted by the aeons of stillness left behind after the departure of these age-old builders.

The avenue down which we padded opened out onto a wide grassy plaza, surrounded by many other such buildings, but bounded on the left and right by the two towering pyramids we had seen earlier. Some figures approached us across this wide lawn. The one in the centre wore a light-coloured suit and a dark tie. He was slender, with a slight stoop to his shoulders and a shock of hair (now white) like a lion's mane—I knew him at once for Lychfield. The others accompanying him were variously dressed—some were natives, others wore European clothing, and red and white faces mingled.

"McCracken!" said Lychfield, with a smile that barely disturbed his lips but sparkled in his eyes a little. He put out a hand and shook mine. "It's been a long time!"

"About fifteen years," I said. "This is my wife, Ariadne."

"Delighted," said Lychfield, shaking her hand. "Welcome to Xulamqamtun, Mrs. McCracken.

Your reputation has preceded you, of course—how is your uncle, Mr. Graham Bell?"

"Thank you. We were in New York to be with him for his first trans-continental telephone call."

"A very great man!" enthused Lychfield. Turning to me, he added, "I'm glad to see you've done so well in marriage, McCracken!"

"I got a good deal," I said. "Unfortunately, Ari has to put up with me. And this is Fritz."

Lychfield nodded briefly. Looking around, he saw that the native servants were carrying our things away across the grassy expanse. "We've set up living quarters in one of the buildings on the further edge of the plaza," he explained. "There's electricity, and running water after a fashion." Leading us after the bearers, he went on, "I confess I'd rather hoped you'd bring your airship."

"The LS3 is in the Ukraine at the moment," I explained. "Rather difficult to get, what with the War and everything."

"Yes," said Lychfield, musing, "that must make everything difficult. It hardly impacts us out here, of course."

"Really?" I replied. "I'd heard there was a U-boat patrolling the Gulf."

Lychfield didn't answer at once. He seemed a little short of breath, and I realized that he was a good bit older than I'd expected—at least, it's always a bit of a shock to see someone again after a long absence. They seem to have changed so much more than you feel you have yourself.

Lychfield flashed a smile at me. "I wouldn't be surprised," he said. "The last news I remember from the War was that the Germans wanted Mexico to join in on their side."

"I haven't heard that," put in Ari.

"Maybe I'm wrong about that," said Lychfield. "Anyway, it doesn't make much difference to our work—we just keep plodding on, you know."

We had reached the far side of the lawn now, and climbed a few steps to a stone terrace before a building of bare stone with a dark doorway but no windows. Guy lines were strung tautly between the top of the wall and the grass, and I plucked one to see how tense it was.

"No roof on the building," Lychfield explained. "We've waterproofed the living quarters with canvas—we have to keep the rains off, and the cool air in. Have you heard about the advances in air-conditioning, McCracken?"

"Wilmer was explaining it to me on the way," I replied.

"Fascinating," said Lychfield. "It makes the ancient buildings as comfortable as home. This building was part of the Ollamaliztli complex."

"All-of-my-listies?" I asked.

"Ollamaliztli," said Ari. "That was the ball-game they played, wasn't it, Professor Lychfield?"

"Yes," confirmed Lychfield. "The object was to push a rubber ball, weighing about six pounds, through a stone hoop about twenty feet off the ground, without using your hands."

"That doesn't sound too easy," I remarked.

"No, the games could go on for hours, even days," said Lychfield. He sighed deeply. "At the end of it, the losing team was sacrificed to Uacmitum Ahau, the Mayan god of the dead."

"Really!" I exclaimed. "Sounds like final exams at Imperial."

"Let's go in, shall we?" Lychfield led us through the doorway, out of the bright sunlight of Mexico and into a modern-looking corridor lit by electric lights. A soft humming sound filled the corridor, and the air was cool—the miracle of air-conditioning! At regular intervals on either side of the corridor were doors, each painted blue, with a brass handle.

"This is where the European and American workers live," explained Lychfield, pushing open a door inscribed with a white number 12. "The Ququmatz live in their own village, of course, but we can accommodate about twenty here. We had to adapt this one, find a double-bed, extend the room just a little and so forth—you're the first married couple in Xulamqamtun in about a thousand years."

"I'm sorry you had to go to so much trouble," I said.

"Well," added Ari, "I think you'll get your money's worth out of us, Professor Lychfield."

"Of course, of course," replied Lychfield, "I never doubted it."

Our bearers had left our luggage in the middle of a sparsely furnished room—just a bed, a wardrobe, a table and chair, and a couple of armchairs. There were no windows, but cool air came in through vents near the floor, and warm air left through vents near the ceiling. It was aided in its journey by a lazily-turning fan.

"There's running water in the bathroom through that door," Lychfield told us, pointing, "as well as showers. Shared, I'm afraid—it's the best we can do. But I think you can demand a little privacy, Mrs. McCracken."

"That would be nice," said Ari.

"Thank you, Professor Lychfield," I said, "this will do nicely."

Lychfield smiled again. "I hope you'll both be comfortable in here. The climate can be . . . oppressive."

"Is that why Mrs. Lychfield didn't come with you?" inquired Ari.

"Poor Clare," lamented Lychfield. "She wanted to be a part of my work, but the climate really is too much for her asthma."

"Where is she now?" I asked.

"She's in our house in London," answered Lychfield. "My work here is almost finished, so we'll be together again soon. Anyway, please join me for dinner tonight."

"Delightful," I said. "What time?"

"Let's see." Lychfield took a gold watch out of his waistcoat pocket and consulted it briefly. "It's a little after five. Shall we say, seven? Will that be enough time to freshen up and rest?"

"I should think so," said Ari. "Thank you."

Lychfield flashed us a quick smile. "In that case, I'll see you at my place—on top of the temple—at seven o'clock this evening. McCracken, it's been magnificent to see you again; and Mrs. McCracken, a pleasure to meet you."

Silence stayed in the room for almost half a minute after he left. Slowly, I turned to face Ari, and raised one eyebrow inquiringly.

"I don't know," she said. "I haven't made up my mind yet. He's quite charming, I admit. Perhaps I haven't seen enough of him yet."

"There's no satisfying you," I remarked, and opened one of our cases in an effort to find some clean clothes.

CHAPTER 9
DINNER CONVERSATION

At a few minutes before seven o'clock, someone tapped on our door, and I opened it to find a native, his face dark, the shadows under his cheekbones darker, standing in the corridor. He wore western clothes—a black suit with faint vertical stripes, a white waistcoat underneath it, a starched collar, and a dark tie. He looked most uncomfortable and unhappy in it.

"Want to see you Prohessor Leech-hilt for dinner now," he said.

"Thank you . . . ?" I left the question of his name in the air, but he didn't seem to understand me. "What can I call you?" I asked. The native's eyebrows met in a frown over the tremendous nose. "Never mind—Ari, it's time to go!" I called.

The native led us back along the corridor and out into the lavender twilight of Xulamqamtun. Long shadows lay across the grass as we crossed the plaza diagonally towards the pyramid on whose top Lychfield dwelt. As we walked, Ari tried out her Mayan on the servant, and they chatted away incomprehensibly the whole time.

"It looks like a Frank Lloyd Wright home," I remarked, staring up at Lychfield's house.

"It does a little," admitted Ari, following my gaze. The sun shone horizontally over the treetops and turned the glass at the peak into a pyramid of fire. And most of the front of the house was made from glass. "His name's Yaotl," she said in a whisper from the corner of her mouth.

"Who?"

She indicated the native servant with her head. I nodded wisely. We had almost reached the foot of the pyramid now. "I hope Lychfield's cook is as good as Fritz," I said. "Fritz has been spoiling me for food."

"It's nice for Fritz to get the night off," said Ari.

"Yes, it is," I replied. "What's he doing, by the way?"

"I think he's learning Mayan cooking from the locals."

"Not from the headhunters, I hope."

"Do you ever think of anything other than food?"

"Well, food and—Great Scott!" I exclaimed. "Is that an inclined plane lift?"

"You mean a funicular railway?" asked Ari. "That's what it looks like." Lychfield had constructed steel rails up the side of the pyramid to his house, and a small carriage, more like a cable car than a railway coach, waited at the low end. Yaotl ushered us into it and closed the door behind us. He pulled a lever, and with a crackle of electricity that made my heart warm, and a faint hum, the teeth of the pinion slotted into the rack and pulled us steadily up the slope of the ancient temple.

"I'm glad to see Lychfield's knowledge of engineering put to good use," I commented, marveling that he seemed so successfully to have tamed the ancient civilization and the jungle to his purpose.

The trees dropped below us, and a saffron sunlight filled the cabin. A moment later, Yaotl eased back on the lever, and the carriage came to a gentle stop at the summit of the temple. We all got out, and Yaotl led us along a terrace to Lychfield's house. The air was cooler up here, and a gentle breeze wafted across the tree-tops.

The house did indeed look as if Frank Lloyd Wright had designed it. The front was all windows, with a stone chimney rising from the further end. The roof wasn't a normal hipped or gabled roof, but slanted away from the windows gently so that all rain (and there must have been plenty of it) would pour down spouts and into a lush garden behind the house. I could see a couple of locals tending coffee bushes along the near side.

"Beautiful house," I remarked.

"A little out of place, don't you think?" said Ari, cocking an eyebrow. At my presumably blank expression, she explained, "A Frank Lloyd Wright house and a funicular railway on a three-thousand-year-old Mayan temple in the middle of the jungle. That's an awkward combination."

"Perhaps," I said with a shrug, "but every ancient city can't be a museum."

Yaotl held the door open and we proceeded inside. We found ourselves in a conservatory that gave us an excellent view of Xulamqamtun and the jungle beyond. The floor was constructed from irregularly-shaped stone slabs. A fireplace—unlit, of course—was set in the further wall, and before this stood a table with places set for three. We could hear the hum of the air-conditioning, and feel the cool air.

"McCracken!" said Lychfield, coming forward and shaking my hand. "Mrs. McCracken, very nice to see you again."

"What a lovely house!" said Ari enthusiastically. "Did you get Frank Lloyd Wright to design it?"

Lychfield shrugged. "It's more in imitation of Frank Lloyd Wright—I made some improvements."

"It gives such a beautiful view of the forest."

"And a great inclined platform lift," I remarked, stabbing my thumb towards the funicular.

"Thank you," said Lychfield with a humble smile. "Remember what we used to say in the old Imperial days? Better living through engineering! Would you like a drink?"

He spoke to Yaotl, who mixed us a couple of cocktails—they tasted like strawberries, but with a faint kick, so I guessed the fruit juice was mixed with vodka. I would have preferred a whisky, but the drink was at least refreshing. Ari took a mango re-fresco.

We stood with our drinks in our hands, watching as the crimson disc of the sun lingered over the leafy horizon. "It is a pleasant view, isn't it?" said Lychfield. "I can't go completely native—I have to have some things around me that remind me of civi-lization. But it's a heart-warming thing to see the forest through glass."

As he spoke, the bottom rim of the sun touched the tops of the trees. Bands of dark green and red lanced out from it through the canopy. It was as if God were performing a chemical experiment on the litmus paper of the trees. We watched in silence for a few moments, while the fiery splendour raged over the tree-tops. I felt Ari's fingers curl around mine, and she said, "Do you remember the sunsets in The-ra?"

I smiled. "This is almost as beautiful," I said.

Then the sun disappeared, and Yaotl lit the lamps.

"Shall we eat?" suggested Lychfield, leading us over to the table.

The main dish consisted of lightly-seasoned chicken with corn and tomatoes. It was delicious, but not the hot and spicy food I would have expected on a Mexican table.

"That's right," Lychfield said in reply to a question from Ari. "I got a grant for this work back in early '13. Actually, it was Wilmer who helped with the grant—he's a financial genius."

"That explains," said Ari thoughtfully, "why you keep him around."

"Why wouldn't I?" responded Lychfield. "He's useful in all sorts of ways. At any rate, after I got that grant, I could hardly stay at Imperial."

"But it was a little drastic, don't you think?" countered Ari, leaning forward on both of her elbows and swirling her refresco around in her glass before taking a sip. "You've left your wife and son for two years. Do you ever get back?"

"You forget, Mrs. McCracken," replied Lychfield with a winning smile, "there's a War on—I can't easily get back to England."

"Have you tried?" I winced inwardly at Ari's interrogation. Setting my whisky down (I'd managed to get a real drink by this time), I nudged her under the table with my foot. She didn't respond, which meant I couldn't flash her a warning signal with my eyes.

Lychfield smiled again, sipped at his strawberry vodka, and said, "I didn't expect at first to be away so long; and now, what with the War, I might not get to return to them until it's all over."

"How did the Rector respond when you turned in your resignation?" asked Ari.

For a second or two, Lychfield's smile was frozen on his lips. Then he said, "Oh, I know what they say about me back at Imperial—that I was forced to leave. Not all faculty-lounge gossip should be taken at face value."

Ari raised her eyebrows. "Is that what they say?" she asked ingenuously. She speared a piece of chicken with her fork and popped it into her mouth.

"What about when you finish here?" I asked, trying to change the subject. "What will you do then?"

Lychfield set aside his drink and picked up his knife and fork. "I don't think the Ivy Leagues are ready for me yet," he said, "but there's a university in Colorado, the School of Mines. It's been around for about forty years now. Perhaps I can teach there."

"So you won't try to open the International Mining Institute?" Ari said, and I gave an internal wince again.

"My, my, Mrs. McCracken," said Lychfield, wiping the corners of his mouth with his serviette and leaning back in his chair, "what a lot you seem to know about me. Yes, Wilmer and I had a plan to open a college of mining in Austria. We still might do that."

"Will you bring your family with you to Austria?" asked Ari.

"I expect so," replied Lychfield. "I expect my son will stay in England—he's to become an actor, apparently." The door opened, and Yaotl entered. "Ah—dessert!" exclaimed Lychfield.

We spent a few minutes praising the truly remarkable dessert—Lychfield called them fried plantains, and they were a bit like crispy bananas, drizzled with caramel and a tangy cream sauce. Even Ari stopped talking for a while. Yaotl returned and poured us each a small cup of espresso. It was bold, and just a tiny bit smoky. I announced my delight with it.

"We grow and roast the beans here," answered Lychfield, smiling modestly. "It's only a small-scale operation, of course." He breathed in the coffee for a moment, then sipped delicately at it. "I think the results are exemplary, though, don't you?" He set the cup down on a little saucer, and a gravity settled over his features. "Well," he said, "this has been very pleasant, but now I think it's time to explain something that is not quite so pleasant."

I straightened in my chair. "Really?" Something important was about to happen—I could tell. In my head, I prayed for the grace to say all the right things and none of the wrong things.

"Do you remember a classmate of yours from Imperial," said Lychfield, "an Italian fellow?"

"Serpe?" I said.

"Yes, that's what all the chaps called him, I think." To Ari, he explained, "His real name was Cristofero Campo di Serpenti."

"Serpe for short," I said. "His father wanted him to study something 'useful,' something that would turn into a career, which is why he was at Imperial."

"A very fine student," interjected Lychfield. "He didn't neglect his studies just because he wanted to study something else."

At Ari's prompting, I went on: "Serpe's real passion was ancient civilizations—you'd like him. After he graduated from Imperial, he went to Oxford and took a first in Classics. Is he all right, Professor?" I asked. "The last I heard, he was teaching ancient civilizations at Padua."

"He was," agreed Lychfield, "which is why I thought of him when I got that grant, two years ago. I made him an offer, and he took a sabbatical year to come out here to Mexico to help me with all these Mayan inscriptions."

"Serpe's here?" I said.

Lychfield drew in a deep breath and held out his coffee cup, which Yaotl refilled. "No," he said. Turning to Ari, he went on, "There is a chamber we discovered fairly early on—we call it the Map Room. The map is on the walls, all frescoes. It's composed of pictures from Mayan mythology and hieroglyphic writing, with a lot of geometric designs. It's full of steles—standing stones, carved with Mayan glyphs. The steles are the key to understanding what's written on the walls, a kind of code. And the walls will tell us where the major shafts have been sunk, how they're connected, and how deep they go. They tell us when the Mayans did most of their mining and why—the Mayans were great astrologers, and didn't do anything unless the heavens spoke to them first. So there's a complex relationship between the glyphs, the frescoes, and the positions of the stars and planets. Cristofero was in the middle of interpreting these for us when he . . . disappeared."

"Disappeared?" I echoed in alarm.

Lychfield nodded. "Yes, just vanished. We haven't a clue where he went. I made inquiries, but nobody has seen anything of him." He loaded his coffee with sugar and whisked the spoon around it so it rattled musically against the sides.

"Is that it?" protested Ari. "You made inquiries—what sort of inquiries? Did he leave any clues?"

In my consternation, I rose from the table and paced over to the window. Xulamqamtun was dark below us, but the stars, which the Mayans had loved and consulted so much, glittered brightly overhead. "When did you notice he was missing?" I asked.

"About six weeks ago," replied Lychfield. "Straight away, we started looking for you—I knew you had married an expert in ancient languages."

"You started looking for his replacement straight away!" exclaimed Ari. "Pardon me, but it sounds like you didn't make much of an effort to find him."

Lychfield stared at the miniscule coffee cup before him. He said, "You have to understand some-

113

thing about the forest here, Mrs. McCracken. You can cut a path with a machete; a day later, it will be overgrown; in two days, no sign you've ever been there will remain. And by the time we found out Cristofero was missing, he'd already been gone for two days."

Ari narrowed her eyes. "Two days!"

"He worked mostly alone," Lychfield told her, "so it was a while before anyone realized he was gone. By the time we noticed, there was no trace of him at all. It's the way of the jungle. I talked to the Ququmatz—I'm not sure I entirely trust them, but I think they were honest in this case. They claim to have seen nothing of him. We also informed the authorities in Campeche, but they have turned up nothing, nothing at all."

"That's terrible," commented Ari. "Is he married?"

"He was," replied Lychfield. "We've informed his wife, of course—or, most likely, we have to say, his widow. But here, the trail is cold."

"Didn't he leave anything behind—possessions, notes, anything like that?" asked Ari. I put my back to the window and returned to the table. Sneaking a glance at Ari, I guessed that she had reached the same conclusion I had—that this was exactly one of those situations we had discussed before leaving Campeche. Time to get out. I sat down.

"Well, yes," replied Lychfield, "he did leave his notes—you'll have full access to them, of course."

Ari blinked. "I wasn't thinking about using them," she said. "I was thinking that there might be a clue in them about where he went."

Now Lychfield blinked a few times. "Of course," he said. "Yes, of course. Well, there's not much in them except his professional notes on the Mayan language and translations of the glyphs in the Map Room. Nothing that would give us a clue as to his whereabouts."

"Did you keep his personal effects?" I asked.

"I'm afraid not," answered Lychfield immediately. "We sent them to his wife."

"But I thought—"

Ari tapped my shin with her toe under the table. "I'm sure you did everything you could," she said reassuringly. She had a little dessert left, and was busy pushing the last couple of plantains onto her fork. It seemed clear to me that she didn't want to pursue the subject any further.

"Professor Lychfield," I said, "thank you very much for this meal. I wish we'd had better news of poor old Serpe. Still, we've had a long day, and we need to get up early to start work tomorrow."

"Of course," said Lychfield, the chair scraping behind him as he stood up. "I hope the coffee doesn't keep you up too long!"

As we stood to leave, Ari said brightly, "Professor Lychfield, perhaps I could have a look at Cristofero's notes now? Studying right before bed seems to fix things in my mind."

Lychfield hesitated a fraction of a second. "Well, I'm not sure I can put my hands on them at this moment. But I'll see you have them first thing tomorrow morning."

A few minutes later, we climbed into the funicular carriage, waving cheerfully at Lychfield. I eased the lever down, and after an initial jolt, it descended the slope smoothly, the electric motor humming as we went. The stars were bright in the sky—you never really see the grandeur of the night sky in a modern city, where gas or electric light swamps most of what God put there. But I wasn't looking at the stars. I was thinking of the intense brown eyes of Cristofero Serpenti.

Ari stood in the front of the carriage, silent and motionless.

The funicular came to a stop in the plaza. We got out. The door clicked shut behind us. The jungle swallowed the sound, as it seemed to swallow everything else, eventually.

We didn't speak until we had reached our room, closed the door, and locked it behind us. Ari turned on the air conditioner, which emitted a loud hum as well as cool air.

"I know what you're going to say," I said, "and I agree. It's very strange that Lychfield couldn't get to Europe to see his family because of the War, but he's able to send Serpe's personal effects to his—to his wife. *I* won't say *widow*."

"And he was so evasive," Ari added, "about everything, but especially about what measures he'd taken to find your friend."

I nodded. "We'll leave at once," I said. "I'll speak to Lychfield tomorrow morning, and tell him we have to leave at once for New York. I'll tell him it's family business."

"But that's not true." Smiling faintly, Ari reached up and kissed me on the lips. "You're very sweet," she said, "and I'd really like to leave right away, but we can hardly do that, can we?" I must have looked confused, because she went on to explain: "Your friend is missing. We have to stay here so we can find him. He might still be alive, and waiting for a rescue. Nobody else will even look for him now. It's up to us." She paused, then added thoughtfully, "Lychfield is certainly trying to hide something. He won't let me see Cristofero's notes. I'd bet anything he wants to look through them himself before he gives them to me." Looking me directly in the eyes, she said, "It wouldn't surprise me to discover that Cristofero had found something Lychfield didn't want found. It wouldn't surprise me at all if Lychfield had somehow gotten rid of him."

I took a deep breath and loosened my tie. "So, let me get this straight," I said. "We have to stay here and look for Serpe, even though he might be dead."

"That's right," said Ari.

I hung up my tie and jacket. "We have to do this right under the nose of the person who probably caused him to disappear. And if Lychfield made Serpe disappear, he could do the same to us."

"That's right," said Ari.

I gave a deep sigh. "Well, I just needed to assess the dangers accurately," I said. "It's going to be very difficult, and very dangerous."

Ari nodded slowly. "That's right," she said. And, although I couldn't be sure of it, I thought I saw a glint in her eye.

CHAPTER 10
BELOW THE TEMPLE

The next morning, Lychfield introduced me to the Foreman, Dean, a slight man who had evidently been trying to grow a little ginger beard for some time. His eyes sparkled with good humour, belying the skeletal way in which his skin seemed to be stretched over his cheekbones, and his lips gave the impression of always being puckered, though I doubted he ever kissed anything.

Dean gave me a quick tour of Xulamqamtun—the parts of it relevant to us engineers, anyway. First, he took me to a stone hut off on the edge of the city. This housed a pair of large machines, on which copper coils were visible, connected by belts to wheels. I could smell the electricity in the air.

"Nice generators," I said. "Where do you get the mechanical power?"

Dean pointed to where a belt, by means of a pair of toothed wheels, disappeared into the ground. "Underground river provides mechanical energy," he said. "It's converted to electricity for the whole camp up here."

"This must generate a lot of electricity," I pointed out, "more than we really need for the camp."

Dean's brow wrinkled. "I built it to the specifications Professor Lychfield gave me," he said. "If we don't need all the electricity we generate, I can just shut down one generator. But actually, that hasn't happened."

We went to the workshop next. It was brand-new, with workbenches that had not yet been dented or scratched, fans that hummed so faintly you were hardly aware that they were on, and new tools, all bright and stored in orderly ranks in drawers and cabinets. They had all the parts for a couple of Pelton turbines, but they're very different from my own patent, which for the sake of compactness uses narrow blades rotating at a high speed like an aeroplane's propeller within a small cage. I could see—and I explained to Dean, though he didn't seem to understand the significance of my words at all—that we'd actually have to manufacture some of the parts from scratch.

I spent most of the morning on the lathe, and as noon approached, had finished a pair of shiny cages, about a foot and a half in diameter. It was like the Creation, in a way. It always is—my work is a prayer, and in a mystical way, God works through me in the workshop. We started with nothing but chaos, but we turned the steel on the lathes, and there was light, and heat, and at the end, two shiny rings connected by a series of slats. And they were good! I left the construction of the pistons that would go through the centre of the blades for the following day.

Over the next few days, a pair of portable water turbines began to take shape in the workshop of Xulamqamtun.

Often, I would eat lunch with Ari in the Map Room. This was a circular room whose walls were covered, as Lychfield had said, with frescoes, and in whose middle stood a kind of Mayan Stonehenge—a wheel of steles, covered with glyphs. Ari sat there at the hub, Serpe's notes and her own and a plethora of reference books spread out like spokes around her. She worked with a pencil in one hand and a magnifying glass in the other.

One day, shortly after our arrival in Xulamqamtun, Fritz came hurrying into the Map Room, carrying a tray on which he had set a large pot of coffee, some cream, brown sugar, and three fat tortillas, oozing with cheese and red peppers. As soon as we were through with Grace, but before we could take a single bite, he blurted out: "Frau McCracken, Herr McCracken—look what I have found."

Fishing in his pocket, Fritz produced a crumpled little red and white box with the word HALPAUS printed on it.

"A cigarette packet, Fritz?" I said doubtfully.

"*Jawohl*, Herr McCracken," replied Fritz animatedly, glancing over his shoulder to see if anyone else were nearby. "But these, they are not just any cigarette—Halpaus is the brand of cigarette most German soldiers smoke. And I found them . . . " He leaned close and whispered conspiratorially, "*here*!"

"In Hoomie-loomie-toon?"

Fritz nodded. "Herr McCracken, I am wondering—who in Xulamqamtun is German? I am German, of course, but who else? Nobody. Who dropped this packet? Somebody."

"Gusta said a U-boat had been seen in these waters," I whispered, leaning close to the others. Nobody spoke for a while. We just munched our tortillas. I could see Ari was avoiding my eye. With a sigh, I said, "So, Lychfield is working with the Germans."

Ari reached out and laid her hand upon mine. "I'm sorry, love," she said.

I didn't say anything for a few moments. Then I looked up into her eyes and gave a lopsided grin. "Well," I said, "now I know why I only got a C in Freshman Geology."

"You mean, only a traitor would give you anything other than an A in a class?" said Ari dubiously.

"Oh, I never got one of those," I answered. "I was hoping for a C+." I picked up the crumpled cigarette packet, crammed it into my carpet bag, and went back to the workshop.

I didn't pay much attention to my work that afternoon. My mind raged over Lychfield's betrayal, and I cooked up one scheme after another for slowing down work on the turbines—anything to frustrate Lychfield's plan. Once, I deliberately slipped while using the lathe and made an irreversible mess of a whole morning's work. It was one of the most difficult things I've ever done.

By late afternoon, I'd settled on a plan that involved finishing my work, then lying in wait along the coast until the U-boat came back. I'd begun figuring out how to contact Gusta and enlist his help, when Lychfield showed up in the workshop to check our progress on the water turbines. He was perfectly charming and genial, and I wanted to punch him right in the middle of his face.

"Afternoon, McCracken," he said, shuffling up to my workbench. "How is the work coming along?"

I put on my best gormless face. "Well, I've made a dreadful mess of one of the pistons, but I'll get back onto it as soon as I can. The cages are finished, but we have to construct new blades—the ones you had for the Pelton turbines aren't the right size or shape."

I suddenly realized, to my horror, that I'd left my carpet bag open on the workbench, and that the cigarette packet was plainly visible. If Lychfield saw it, he would know that we were onto him; but he was between me and the carpet bag.

"Are you managing to follow all this, Dean?" Lychfield asked over his shoulder. Dean hurried up to my workbench. "The blades we bought were the wrong size and shape."

"Have you been making plans?" Dean asked.

"I can draw some up this afternoon," I said. "Do you have any blueprint paper?" I tried to edge around Lychfield towards my carpet bag.

"We have some paper, some ferro-gallate, and some glass over here—let me show you," Dean said.

"Well, I won't need it at once," I replied, taking a small step closer to the carpet bag. To cover my movement, I straightened a few of the tools I'd been using on another workbench.

"I'll leave the two of you to settle this," said Lychfield. "This is good progress, so far." Reaching out, he gathered the handles of my carpet bag and slid it under the workbench. "You probably want this out of the way," he said, and left.

Had he seen the cigarette packet? I wondered. Was he just good at concealing his reactions? Would I find myself walking to my room one night, and feel the soft drowsiness of a chloroform pad over my face? When I returned to our room that night, my eyes darted back and forth, and I took constant glances over my shoulder.

The next evening, we started searching the mineshafts and chambers below Xulamqamtun for signs of Serpe. We knew where the entrance was, of course—Lychfield and Wilmer and Dean made no secret of that—but now Ari had made enough progress with decoding the glyphs that she could begin drawing a rudimentary map.

The sun went down that night, and a sleepy silence settled over the Mayan ruins—as much silence as the jungle could manage, that is. Even in our room, we could hear the rhythmic creaking of the frogs and the insects, the occasional cries of the night creatures, God's great factory for constructing life, all around us. We waited an hour, our eyes shining in the darkness, until we were certain that everyone was asleep, then we rose quietly and emerged into the corridor. I pushed open the door at the far end, and we stepped out into the blue and silver night of Xulamqamtun.

Fritz was waiting for us, with cups of hot chocolate. It was especially good in Mexico, I reflected, carrying just a hint of cinnamon, nutmeg, and (oddly delicious) cayenne pepper. I sipped at my cup and we set off across the plaza towards the Map Room.

The buildings were dark silhouettes all around us. At the top of the temple, a single light showed that Lychfield was still awake, but everything else was dark, as it had been for a thousand years since the Mayans left their cities, their astronomical charts, their steles, and their lives. Black shapes loomed out of the darkness ahead of us—the monuments that flanked the dim entrance to the Map Room. Ari pushed open the door, and we went inside.

We switched on our electric torches. The shadows of the glyphs reeled and bounced all around us as we made our way to the far side of the room.

"Here I will stay, Herr and Frau McCracken," said Fritz, taking his position as we had planned. "If anything I hear, I will at once find you."

"We're going to explore the yellow passages tonight," Ari explained. "Just follow the yellow markers above the doorways, and you should be able to find us."

"Yellow?" I asked, as we entered the passageway at the back of the Map Room.

Ari flashed her torch up at the lintel. The top was daubed with flaking yellow paint. "The Mayans associated each of the compass-points with a different colour," she told me. "Yellow for east—the most important direction, because that's where the sun rises—and red for the north, black for south, and white for west. Green or blue was for the centre—it was important for the Mayans to find the centre, so that the gods of the four compass points could combine their blessings and give them strength." She shone her light on a picture of a young man paddling a canoe, surrounded by sea-birds. "That's Kinich Ahau, the Mayan god of the sun." The passageway went on for about twenty yards, then opened out into a small room with a door in each wall. I looked up and headed towards the yellow lintel.

"So they used the colours down here to tell you which direction you were going?" I said.

"That's right," Ari confirmed. "If you got proper directions, you'd never get lost—someone would tell you to go two yellows, a black and a red, and you'd always end up in the same place." She pointed. "Yellow again," she suggested.

Steps descended from the door, and the pools of brown light cast by our torches bobbed and darted ahead of us, but never found the bottom.

"How deep does this go?" I wondered.

"As deep as you're comfortable with, and then a little more," answered Ari.

A moment later, the circles of torchlight struck a sandy floor, and we found ourselves in a wide room whose walls were covered with pictures. Ari shone her light on them and wandered slowly along the walls, her lips moving silently as she interpreted the signs.

I looked at the rest of the room. There were three doors, each with a coloured lintel as before. But the room was completely empty, the floor covered with an even layer of sand. I turned to Ari. "What do these pictures tell you?" I asked.

"They're just pictures—pictures of things." I looked, and saw pictures of golden thrones and tables, arm-rings studded with precious stones, knives with jeweled handles, jaguars with emerald eyes and silver claws, carved stone statues of kings and queens and artisans. "Look," said Ari, pointing, "there's Kinich Ahau again."

"He looks a lot older there," I observed.

"That was one of the forms he took—the young man in the canoe was another, and the other was a sea-bird—look, there's a couple of sea-birds and a boy in a canoe. And there's a litter for carrying rich people around the city, and candlesticks, and armour and shields." She frowned. "But there's no order to it—it doesn't seem to tell a story. There are no repeating characters." Her eyes widened. "Wait," she said slowly, turning on her heel and shining her light on each of the other walls in turn. Finding what she apparently wanted, she strode across the room. She flashed her light on a series of complicated figures that were placed in squares, from ceiling to floor, in three columns. Her lips moved again for a few moments, then she took out a notebook, consulted it a few times, and scribbled a note. At the end of it, she caught her breath and made the Sign of the Cross.

"Is it a curse?" My mouth was dry.

"No," replied Ari, "or, yes—it is. It's a curse on whoever removes the contents of this room, but it also explains that the walls are . . . well, I suppose the best word we have would be *inventory*."

I turned round, shining my light over the pictures, awe growing in my heart. "Great Scott!" I said. "You mean these are pictures of things that were once in this room?"

"Yes, and there's a curse on anyone who removes anything—he will incur the wrath of Kinich Ahau, and the eastern sea will swallow him up."

"I didn't touch a thing," I protested.

"No, but someone did."

"Looters?" I suggested. I knew there was a black market for Mayan artifacts; looters were the scourge of archaeologists everywhere.

"Could be," Ari admitted. "But this is very much more careful and thorough than the work of any looters I've heard of before. This room has been stripped systematically—looters aren't well organized, and they're not careful. They break things, they leave things behind they think they can't sell, and what they leave behind is always in disarray. They scuff up the ground, light fires, and leave traces of the food they've eaten. There would be footprints all over. But this looks as if it has been swept clean."

"I bet Lychfield has cleaned these rooms out," I said, bitterly—I was prepared to believe the worst about him now, so long as it was the truth. But then a thought suddenly struck me. "I have it," I said. "There's a U-boat near here—Lychfield is digging up Mayan treasure to give to the Germans. War is expensive, and I've heard Germany is getting short of cash—all this Mayan gold is going to help the Kaiser's war effort!"

"That must be it," replied Ari. "But where is Lychfield keeping all this stuff? I haven't seen a hint of it in Xulamqamtun."

"Shshhh!" I hissed, holding a finger to my lips. I darted over to the door we had come through (it was painted white on the inside), thumbing off the torch. Ari did the same, plunging us into darkness.

Hurried footsteps scuffled and clattered on the stairs, and I could see the wavering light of an electric torch.

"Someone's coming," I said, rather uselessly. "Where can we hide?"

"One of the passageways?" suggested Ari. I turned on my torch, and we dashed over to the red door.

"There's a two-thirds chance he won't come this way," I said, extinguishing my torch.

"It might be Fritz," Ari pointed out.

I peered out through the doorway into the dark of the chamber. It was the darkest thing I'd ever seen. If you close your eyes, there's usually enough light to shine through your eyelids. But here there was nothing. I might have been staring into the abyss before the Creation.

And then there was light.

For a moment, the doorway framed the yellow light, and then it became the wavering spot of a torch. Some of it spilled backwards and upwards, revealing a pair of weird eyes and tousled, reddish hair.

Thumbing on my torch, I stepped out into the chamber. "Hello there, Fritz!" I said cheerfully.

"*Ach!*" exclaimed Fritz, jumping so badly that he dropped his torch and it went out. "Herr McCracken," he said, when he had recovered, "to find you is good, *ja*?" I shone the light on the floor so he could find his torch. Fritz went on, "There are men—they come here, through the passageways, down the steps. I keep track of them from in front. It is very difficult, but I do it."

"How far back are they?" asked Ari.

"Not much far," replied Fritz. He stopped and cocked his head. "Here they come," he said, and we all hurried back into the passageway where we had hidden before. Out went the lights.

Then the men entered the chamber. There were three of them, and they all carried oil lamps. They wore the white naval uniforms, jackboots and black sailors' hats of the *Kaiserliche Marine*. They chattered among themselves as they went, oblivious to our existence.

Nevertheless, to my horror, they turned towards us.

Ari and Fritz saw what was happening, and there was a fragment of a second during which everybody was too horrified to make a decision. Then we all turned and strode away from the oncoming sailors, trying to keep just ahead of the light their lanterns spilled.

The German sailors walked quite briskly, and we had almost to run to keep ahead of them. But whereas they had light to guide them, we had to run through the thick darkness of the Mayan mines. If one of us stumbled, the light from their lamps would instantly have revealed us.

The Germans laughed as they chatted with each other. We strode on ahead, our eyes glancing backwards from time to time, praying frantically in our heads, our fingertips tapping the walls because we couldn't see the doors and passageways before our faces. Ahead of me, I could just hear Fritz panting, and occasionally muttering.

A moment later, I found a corner. We followed the turn a little way, but I paused and turned to watch our pursuers.

It wasn't a turn in the passageway. We had happened upon another chamber, and the sailors were now moving away from us, towards another door in the far wall.

I muttered a short prayer of thanks—we had not been discovered. Then I reached out and grabbed Fritz by the shoulder. Leaning close to his ear, I whispered, "Now let's follow them!" I reached out for Ari and whispered the same thing.

It was a lot easier to follow them than to be followed. They made a lot of noise, and the light painted the sides of the passageway, the floor and the ceiling all with its golden glow.

"What are they saying?" I asked Fritz, hoping to get some kind of clue about Lychfield's plans.

"They talk of beer and home," Fritz whispered back.

So much for that, then. We strode on ahead, keeping the glow of their lanterns squarely ahead of us.

After a little while, the passageway opened up once more into a wide chamber—the German lamplight formed a kind of globe around the sailors without striking any walls, and the ground was more uneven than it had been. We could hear the sound of running water some way ahead. I reached out and stayed Fritz and Ari, then cautiously switched on my torch for a moment.

The light picked out a pile of rock, a sharp, irregularly-shaped cone that was a pale greenish in colour, directly in front of us. I gathered Fritz and Ari towards me as if we were in a small rugby huddle, and said, "We seem to be in a cavern of some kind."

"Yes," said Ari, "that's a stalagmite. Let's carry on following the Germans."

But before we were able to continue our pursuit of the sailors, a voice came to us out of the darkness to our right.

"Cracky!" said the voice in a delighted tone. "*Buongiorno!*"

CHAPTER 11
GOLD FOR THE KAISER

Three electric torch beams sliced through the darkness and concentrated on the place the voice had come from. There, behind a set of iron bars dripping with water and rusting, was a grubby face with disarranged hair, round spectacles, and a small beard. In the midst of the grime, the corners of the mouth turned upwards, revealing bright teeth.

"Serpe!" I exclaimed, rushing over to the bars and clutching them tightly.

"Cracky!" replied Serpe. "*Mamma mia,* how good it is to see you, *vecchio amico*!" Reaching between the bars, he grasped my hand, and we shook. Instantly, he broke out into song: "We are, we are, we are, we are, we are the engineers!"

"We can, we can, we can, we can demolish forty beers!" I sang back. And we both finished the verse: "Drink rum, drink rum, drink rum—"

"Are you mad, or what?" hissed Ari, leaping forward between us. She jabbed a finger. "There's a shipload of Germans down there, and you want to sing drinking songs?"

"Well, technically not a shipload," I answered. "The full complement of a modern U-boat is . . . "

135

At Ari's expression, I hung my head sheepishly, but Serpe, if anything, perked up.

"Cracky," he said, "is this *bella donna* your lady wife?" He reached out, took Ari's hand, and kissed it through the bars. "She is very beautiful, Cracky—not as beautiful as my Maria, but very beautiful nonetheless."

"Ariadne, my wife," I said. "Cristofero Serpenti, or just Serpe to his friends." Bringing Fritz forward, I introduced him too.

"*Guten Abend*, Herr Serpe," said Fritz with a nod of his head.

"My heart is delighted to meet you both," said Serpe. "You and I, Fritz, I think we should be enemies—even now, our peoples fight in the mountains in the north of my beloved *patria*."

"Then I am glad we are not there, Herr Serpe," replied Fritz.

"I am glad also we are not there, Signor Fritz," said Serpe. "Here, at least, good sense can rule instead of insanity."

"How have you been Serpe?" I asked.

"How have I been?" He shrugged and opened his hands wide. "Not so good, Cracky. In a dungeon. That is almost as bad as it can be, I think, eh?"

"Not so good, all right," I said. "Why haven't you broken out?"

"It is not so easy, I think," answered Serpe. "They build these places so a man cannot get out. I have tried. It is very discouraging. But I find things to do here, you know." I shone my torchlight through the bars of his dungeon, but could see nothing except a dirty straw pallet. "I have been working on a few problems," Serpe went on. "On my first day in this place, I saw a snake—you know, a big one, about so long." He held his hands about three feet apart. "And then, *mio amico*," he said, leaning closer and speaking confidentially as if imparting the secrets of the Eleusinian Mysteries, "and then I am remembering my Philostratus. You remember, Cracky, how he is describing Ajax as having a pet snake? This snake is eating and drinking with Ajax all the time, following him around like a dog. So, I think, if Ajax, *quel bellimbusto stupido*, if he can train a snake, then why cannot Cristofero Campo di Serpenti train a snake also? Maybe, I am thinking, this snake can carry messages to the surface. Perhaps there is someone up there who can rescue me."

"Did you manage to train the snake?" I asked.

Serpe spread his hands. "No, but here you are anyway. You came without the snake. *Deus providavit*."

I ran my eye over the bars, up and down and across at the top and bottom. "I just bet we can do something to get you out of here, Serpe," I said.

"I wish you would," replied Serpe. "It is very terrible in here."

"It will not take long, Herr Serpe," said Fritz, drawing his Mauser and aiming at the lock.

Serpe narrowed his eyes. "You know, Fritz, your voice is not the first German voice I have heard in Xulamqamtun. There are many *Tedeschi* here—I have seen them many times, but I tell the Professor nothing." He laid a finger to his lips to confirm his silence. "Not a word, though I see them passing by in secret many times. Serpe's eye is sharp, you see! Then, one time, I see the Professor speaking with . . . what is the English word? . . . *ufficiale* in the *Marina Tedesca.*"

"An officer in the German Navy?" translated Ari.

"*Si, appunto!*" enthused Serpe. "*Era il capitano di un sottomarino.* How is that in English?"

"A U-boat captain," I said. I didn't need a translation of that.

"*Si,*" said Serpe. "This Professor Liccifieltro, he is a traitor—worse than Brutus, worse than Cassius! He is with them in the mouth of Satan. All this Mayan gold he has discovered—he will pass it on to the Germans. I heard him discussing this with the captain of the *sottomarino.* With this money, the Kaiser, he will go on fighting for many more months. Many more Englishmen, and Frenchmen, and Italians will die as the fighting, it goes on and on. But alas, when I see these two talking together, they also see me, and *boom!* I am in a dungeon below . . . " His voice faded away, and his eyes fixed on a point some distance off, past my right shoulder. Ari, Fritz and I spun around.

There, in our combined torchlight, stood Lychfield, Wilmer, and Dean. Each of them held a lantern in one hand, and a Luger in the other. Lychfield wore, I noticed, a pair of white gloves.

"My dear Cristofero," said Lychfield, his voice mild as always, "I do hope you haven't been too lonely down here. It seems, at any rate, that you'll have some companionship now. Mr. Dean, would you please open the door to the dungeon and let Mr. and Mrs. McCracken and their odd friend in? Search them first."

Wilmer moved over to Ari, but Lychfield stopped him. "Hands off, Wilmer. Dean, you search them."

Dean set down his lantern, stepped forward and patted each of us down. He removed a revolver and a pair of knuckle-dusters from Ari's pockets, a Bowie knife from my own and a stiletto from Fritz's.

"I think she has a derringer in her blouse," observed Wilmer, pointing at Ari.

"Good eye, Wilmer," observed Lychfield. "If you please, ma'am—slowly and carefully."

Ari reached into her blouse and drew her derringer, holding it between her thumb and forefinger. She dropped it into Dean's palm, and he handed the cache over to Wilmer, who stuffed his own pockets with the contraband.

"No Mauser, Fritz?" I asked in a whisper.

"Not tonight, Herr McCracken," whispered Fritz in reply, and he made an odd gesture with his head. I fell silent.

Dean, meanwhile, had rattled some keys in the lock, and now he waved us into the dungeon with the barrel of his gun. We went in without demur, the keys rattled again, and we were imprisoned. I grasped the bars so tightly that I could see my knuckles whiten in the light of the lanterns. "So much for the water turbines," I commented bitterly.

"Yes, I had hoped we might get a little more gold out of the mines with your help, McCracken, but never mind—your efforts have helped the Kaiser quite enough, I think."

"*Kaiser Wilhelm ist ein Angebar und Feigling!*" shouted Fritz, surprising me with his vehemence as he waved his fists at them through the bars.

Lychfield smiled silently, contemplating Fritz the while, and slowly he pocketed his Luger. "I'm sure the Kaiser is a braggart and a coward," he said, and he almost sounded reasonable, "but he's also a visionary, and with this gold, he'll soon be ruling the former British Empire." He smile widened. "It looks as if the sun will finally set on it," he concluded.

"And what part of the Empire do you get for your services, Lychfield?" I asked, unable to suppress the sneer in my voice.

Lychfield turned to Wilmer and Dean. "You know what to do," he said. "I won't be long." Nodding their obedience, they departed, their lanterns dwindling as they got further away. Lychfield watched where they had gone thoughtfully for a moment, then set his lantern down near our cell and, finger by finger, pulled off his gloves. He reached into the breast pocket of his jacket, drew out a packet of Halpaus cigarettes, and lit one from the lantern flame. He drew in a deep lungful—I could smell its acrid smoke, and my nose wrinkled—and blew it out over his shoulder. "I used to smoke when I was an undergraduate," he mused. "I don't any more, of course, but Captain Schultz gave me these. I will enjoy them over a very long time, I think." His musing over, he looked up at his prisoners. "You'll be surprised, McCracken, to discover that I don't get any share of the Empire at all. Not so much as a square foot of the remotest corner of it."

"I understand, Lychfield," said Ari, coming forward to the bars and thrusting her face between them. "This is your revenge—for being rejected by your fellow professors at Imperial."

Lychfield smoked in silence for a while, the blue cloud throwing a slight haze over the lantern. At last, he said, "I confess, it will be a splendid moment when those tweed-jacketed dimwits see my successes and measure them against their own pointless lives. What a name for a school! Imperial! As if the Empire is the only thing in the world, or as if it will last for ever! Will they, I wonder, retain that name when the Empire has fallen?"

"You must have felt so hurt when they fired you," observed Ari, her voice dropping.

"Oh, don't think you can get me that way, Mrs. McCracken," answered Lychfield. "My firing just confirmed for me what a fool the Rector was." His puffing on the cigarette grew quicker for a few moments. "There will be, I suppose, a certain satisfaction on seeing that idiot's face when he realizes what a mistake he made, but no, that wouldn't be even close to my main motive. Why should I concern myself with fools? They are beneath my contempt—I hardly think of them any more, not the Rector, nor any of those fools who used to laugh behind my back in the faculty lounge. Never to my face, of course—they didn't have the nerve for that. Cowards, as well as fools. But I think of them not at all, dupes and milksops and liars that they were."

"I suppose, then," I interjected, "that you'd betray your country for the sheer villainous pleasure of it all?"

Lychfield laughed, tipping his head back as he did so. He took another drag on the cigarette. "If it comes to treachery, what have I really betrayed? A failing monarchy, the slave of its parliament—of lesser men, elected by a lot of unwashed, ignorant drones. Who is Campbell-Bannerman, anyway?

Some dreadful reformer who's too afraid to be an imperialist or a socialist!"

"Your information is out of date, Lychfield," I said. "Campbell-Bannerman isn't Prime Minister any more."

"Oh, and who is, then? Herbert Asquith? David Lloyd-George? Who are they, compared with William the Conqueror, or Richard the Lion-heart, or Henry V? Compared with men who knew what they wanted, and took it? Kaiser Wilhelm knows what a king ought to be—he wills it, and it happens. He doesn't have to listen to his wretched people; they just do what he tells them. If you're right, you don't have to have the approval of a lot of old women who don't even have an original idea on their favourite beer or sixpenny novel. Kaiser Wilhelm knows the only effective form of government available."

"I didn't know you were a political idealist," I observed with irony.

"Oh, this is not about politics," replied Lychfield airily, "I just need you to understand that I haven't betrayed anyone. Everything I've done has been a statement consistent with my philosophical vision."

"Philosophical vision?"

"Yes, a vision of the future. A vision of better lives through engineering—through mining. This planet abounds in material wealth, just below the surface. And we can rule that wealth by mining it. Let's turn our backs on the superstitions of the past, on the poetry and philosophy and art, knock down the temples, the cathedrals, reduce the inefficiency of the old world to rubble. Then the dawn will arise on a new world—a new dawn of factories, of machines. Imagine, with a mineshaft sunk every mile, we could rip out everything useful from the earth, every last atom, and feed it to our machines. The earth will bend to our will, one giant factory."

"One giant factory," mused Serpe. "I see that we will not rule this new world—you will rule it. It is you who will be its king, its *imperator* unchallenged, I think."

Lychfield nodded energetically, his eyes gleaming in the light cast by the lantern. "Yes, I will. Mining is the door to the new future, and I am the key. I remember those dolts well enough, how they would laugh at my ideas—not just at Imperial, but when I was an undergraduate, the professors of poetry and music and the rest of that rubbish. Well, they'll all be silent in this new world. They won't be able to raise their idiotic voices. The factories will drown them out—*my* factories."

I looked down at the fingers of Lychfield's gloves, which hung out of the hip pocket of his jacket. "I can't imagine you'll dirty your own hands with all this work, though," I argued. "Who will you get to do the actual work?"

"Does it matter? The drones. The surplus population. Didn't your Jesus say, 'The poor you will always have with you?' Now *there* was a visionary statement—he might as well have said, 'The workforce you will always have with you.'"

"You're insane," observed Ari.

"Well, that would be the judgment of the mediocre person," answered Lychfield with a slow nod. "All visionaries must appear insane to their less remarkable contemporaries. Adam Smith looked insane to those unable to see his vision. So did Richard Arkwright. So does Andrew Carnegie. But they saw what the others couldn't see—the new order, the technological order! Men and machines working together!"

"It sounds more like men will be the machine's slaves," Ari commented.

"Some men," replied Lychfield. "What's wrong with that? Some men were meant to serve—didn't Aristotle say, some men were natural slaves? That's not too different from the words of your fellow Jesus." For a few moments, he watched me silently, puffing on his cigarette and blowing the smoke into the cell. I've never enjoyed cigarette smoke—it irritates my throat, and smells awful. But I wouldn't give him the pleasure of seeing me choke, so I put up with it. The orange tip of the cigarette glowed and dulled as he smoked and contemplated. At last, he said, "I had thought, McCracken, that as an engineer you might share this vision. You might have had a role—a minor role, at least above the drones if not

145

quite on my level—in the new technological order. But I see you've been corrupted, perhaps from your more liberally-educated wife. You're far too attached to irrelevant notions like religion, patriotism, chivalry. Good and evil. It's a pity, really." He drew one last lungful of smoke, dropped the butt and ground it under his foot.

"Professor Lychfield," said Ari, "it doesn't have to be like this, you know. You and your ideas are not the same. We don't reject you when we reject your ideas. It's possible to love someone, even when his ideas are bad."

"What a strange idea," said Lychfield in his mildest professorial manner. "What is a man, if not the sum of his ideas? The Kaiser and I have a vision, and he will make it into a reality." He smiled. "First, though, I have to load the gold onto our boats and get it to the U-boat." He turned and started to depart after Wilmer and Dean.

"Why do you keep Wilmer around?" asked Ari, her words sounding abrupt and urgent.

"Because he has a talent for organization," replied Lychfield with utmost reasonableness. "And he's a financial genius, as I told you—he got me my 'grant.' I couldn't have done it without him."

"But he has his flaws too," countered Ari. "You know what I mean—you wouldn't let him search me. He's more of a liability than anything else. But you keep him around anyway. And Dean—he has no personality at all. He can never share your vision, only do your will. If you keep them around, despite their flaws, then might not the rest of us accept you in spite of yours?"

Lychfield stood for a long moment staring at Ari. I began to wonder if her words hadn't struck him to the heart. His hand fluttered to his breast pocket, as if he would have liked to smoke another cigarette. But in the end he just pulled on his gloves again. "What strange notions you have, Mrs. McCracken," he said. "Wilmer and Dean are useful to me, and I'll keep them around only so long as they remain so. As for me—well, within my realm, within the realm of mining, I have no flaws. When the world is one huge mine, the world will acknowledge that fact."

"So you're not keeping any of the gold?" I asked sarcastically.

Lychfield paused and looked around. "Of course I'll keep some," he said. "Some will go to the Kaiser, and some to Pancho Villa."

"Pancho Villa?" said Serpe in surprise. "Why must you give gold to that revolutionary?"

Lychfield shrugged. "Politics, you know," he explained. "A necessary evil. Sinking the *Lusitania* has made Germany very unpopular in America. So the Kaiser believes that funding Pancho Villa's rebellion in Mexico and encouraging him to—ahem—consider alternative military objectives, perhaps in

147

Texas and New Mexico, will keep America busy and out of the War until Germany can beat the English and the French. But that's beyond my scope. It's the other part of the plan that is—if you'll pardon the pun—all *mine*."

With that, he departed. The light of his lantern receded with him, and the darkness closed in all around us.

I pulled at the bars of our cell. I was hoping that there would be some tiny movement in them, indicating a structural weakness in the way they were attached to the floor and ceiling. They didn't budge. But I didn't give up hope—I pulled at them again. They didn't budge again.

"All right, then," I said, turning around— Lychfield had left Serpe with a lantern and he now lit it so that we could at least see each other. "Dean didn't find this." I slid Rob Roy's dirk out of my boot. "What else didn't he find?"

"I have this." Ari reached into her boot and drew out a long stiletto knife. "And this." Pulling off her hairband, she revealed it to be a concealed garrote. "And this." She drew a dirk out of her other boot. Then she slid the heel off her boot and held up a pair of shiny bottles, each about an inch long. "Compressed tear gas," she explained. "Oh, and these too." From the heel of her other boot, she took out two small orange sticks half the size of my little finger. "Small charges of TNT," she said.

"Where did you get all that?" I asked incredulously.

"From the same nice man in New York City who sold Fritz his Mauser."

"I love you," I said admiringly. "Do we have anything else?"

"Nothing much," said Serpe, "but I do have this." He held up a large pistol with a magazine bulging in front of the trigger.

"Where did you get that?" I asked in astonishment.

"To him I passed it behind my back when Herr Lychfield arrived," said Fritz, almost apologetically, as he retrieved his beloved Mauser from Serpe.

"So, when you said you didn't have your Mauser with you tonight—"

"It was literally true at that moment, Herr McCracken," replied Fritz primly. "Perhaps to get out of this cell we can use the Mauser?"

We all retired to different corners of the cell and covered our ears as Fritz leveled the barrel of the Mauser at the lock of the cell door. The flash of light almost blinded us, and the crash of the gun was deafening in the confined space, even though we had covered our ears. The lock leaped a little, and the door creaked open half an inch. I pushed it gently, and it swung wide open.

"They will have heard that," I commented. "Let's get out of here before someone turns up."

The German sailors and Lychfield had disappeared down a passageway marked by a yellow lintel, and we paused by that opening, listening intently.

"Is anyone coming?" asked Ari.

"*Jawohl*, Frau McCracken," confirmed Fritz. "I hear the feet of men—perhaps two, perhaps three. They are coming towards us. We have perhaps half a minute."

"Time to get busy," I said, and quickly outlined a plan. We flattened ourselves against the wall on either side of the yellow-painted doorway. Someone entering the room through that door would have to turn around to see us. Serpe put out the light.

A moment later, half a dozen German sailors entered the chamber, Lugers drawn. One of them held a lantern. They paused before the cell, and the NCO tried the door. It opened easily, of course. He turned to issue orders.

Then he saw us.

Right away, Ari's arm moved. Something flashed silver in the light of the Germans' lantern—one of Ari's tear gas canisters. It hit the ground right in the middle of the sailors and shattered. With a loud hissing noise, a grey cloud rose from it. The Germans cried out in fear, gasping and clutching their throats, their eyes bulging. They tried to get away from the gas, but just lurched into one another. The German carrying the lantern dropped it, and we were all plunged into darkness.

We didn't stop for anything else. My eyes had already begun to run, and I felt as if I were breathing fire. We took to our heels down the yellow passageway. We ran blind, but a faint luminescence glowed from ahead of us. We ran on, away from the grey cloud expanding through the darkness and away from the retching noises of the sailors.

After a few moments, we reached a junction where three passageways met, and we paused.

"Which way?" asked Ari.

"This way," I said, pointing down a red passageway.

"How do you know?"

"There's a faint light shining on the ceiling of that one," I pointed out, "but also that smell of rotten eggs is coming from down there. My guess is hydrogen sulphate—very common in underground rivers. I bet there's a big natural cave there, and Lychfield is using it to store his gold."

'To store his gold," said Serpe, as we began to jog down the red passageway, "but perhaps, I think, something more. The Yucatan Peninsula, it is crisscrossed back and forth with underground rivers and caves. Perhaps it is that Lychfield uses these rivers to move his gold out to the *sottomarino*."

Almost immediately, we knew he was right, because the light began to grow, into a harsh, white light. In a moment more, the passageway opened up onto an amazing sight.

It was indeed a natural cave, shaped a bit like a tube station in London. It stretched away to our left and right. We had emerged onto a wide, flat ledge, higher than the floor of the cave, so that the roof was not far above our heads. The walls were the colour of sand, and hung with stringy stalactites, but the overwhelming impression one got was of blueness. This was because a river, a deep sapphire in colour, ran through the middle of the cave, like the rails in the tube station. On the river were three boats, long and flat-bottomed, with waist-high gunwales. Each was loaded with Mayan gold. The whole cavern was illuminated by halogen lamps suspended from the ceiling. Ventilation was provided by air-conditioning ducts and extractor fans positioned near vents. I pointed the lights and fans out to Ari. "This is why Lychfield needed such a large generator," I said with some satisfaction.

The four of us crept close to the brink of the ledge. It was fringed with stalagmites, behind which we could conceal ourselves from the sight of anyone below.

Below our feet was a dock, to which one of the boats was moored. Into this a team of Ququmatz overseen by Dean was loading the last items of the treasure. I looked at the two boats that bobbed in the middle of the river. Lychfield stood in the lead boat, accompanied by a couple of German sailors, including one who wore a captain's cap. Wilmer was in the other, with another pair of German sailors.

"Is that Ixchel?" asked Ari in a whisper. I looked up. On the other side of the river, and roughly level with our ledge, was the statue of a woman. A snake coiled about her head. In her hands she held a jug, from which issued a stream of water that trickled down a cut in the cliff below, and thence into the river. Years of cascading water had stained the rock there a deep obsidian black.

"*Si, Signora,*" whispered Serpe. "Ixchel, the Lady of Waters, and wife of Kinich Ahau, in one of her less terrifying forms." He pointed. "Look—you see there the remnant of an arch? When the Mayans came here, they built a bridge across the river, and placed Ixchel there."

"To bless their voyages?" asked Ari.

But Serpe shook his head. "Not to bless their voyages," he said. "It is much more likely that they would pray to her to keep the water sweet."

"Right," agreed Ari.

I pointed off to our left. "I think the water used to be much higher," I said. At the far end of the cavern, the river passed out through a natural arch of rock into another cavern, which was also lit by halogen lamps. At the very top of the arch, the rock was the same sandy colour as the rest of the cavern. Below that, however, it was dark, almost black. "Hydrogen sulphate leaves a black residue if it's in a water suspension," I explained. "For many years, it looks like the water came very much higher than it does now."

"Why would that change?" wondered Ari.

I leaned out a little over the edge and peered off to our right. There, at the other end of the cavern, I saw exactly what I had expected to see: a pair of wooden gates, with a sluice gate at the bottom. A narrow ribbon of water spouted through the sluice gate and down a slope to the river below. Above the sluice gate was a platform with a railing, reached by a flight of steel steps. On the platform, a pair of German sailors manned a Maxim MG08 machine gun, mounted on the railing.

"How typical of Professor Lychfield," I said. "He dreams of factories and of lives made better by machines, and here he's turned a river into a canal, with a lock and all. He's stuck in the Industrial Revolution."

"Excuse me, Herr McCracken," said Fritz, "but what is *lock*? I think of keys and locks in doors, not in rivers."

"A lock is a device for raising and lowering the water level in a canal," I explained. "In the Industrial Revolution, British engineers built canals all over England for transporting industrial goods. Locks allowed their boats to get up and down hills quickly and cheaply. No portage for them!"

The roar of an outboard motor filled the cave, and I saw that Lychfield, in the lead boat, had just pulled the starter cord. He lowered the propeller into the water, and edged the raft towards the arch.

"Ach!" exclaimed Fritz. "There is one boatload of gold for that oaf Wilhelm!"

The smells of oil and petrol wafted up to us from below. Lychfield advanced the boat very cautiously. He seemed barely to be moving. The archway was narrow, and the slightest miscalculation would rip up the hull and send all that gold to the bottom of the river. That was good—it would give us a little time to accomplish our plan.

Serpe looked left and right, as I had done, along the river to the archway in one direction and the lock in the other. "Signora McCracken," he said, "do you remember the Mayan myth of Xpiyacoc and Xmucane?"

Ari nodded. "The gods made people out of wood, but they refused to worship them."

"The wooden people, they refused to worship the gods," Serpe went on, "so the gods are sending a flood to destroy them." Smiling, he pointed towards the lock. "If somehow we could blow up the lock, such a deluge would, I think, destroy those who also refuse to worship God!"

"I have TNT," said Ari, "but they're small charges—I don't think they would blow up that lock, even together."

I sniffed the air. "I can't smell the hydrogen sulphate any more," I said.

"Perhaps it came from somewhere else," suggested Ari.

"No, it works on your olfactory organs," I explained. "Small concentrations smell like rotten eggs, but in large concentrations it actually deadens your sense of smell."

"Are you saying that we can't smell it any more because there's actually more of it?" said Ari doubtfully.

I shrugged. "That's science," I said. "I don't make it up, I just work for the Chap who did." I pointed. "Professor Lychfield has lowered the level of the river in the main cave by raising it up there, beyond the lock. And that's where the hydrogen sulphate will be most concentrated." I gave a short dramatic pause. "Hydrogen sulphate is highly flammable—explosive, in a confined space. It would take only a small charge of TNT to ignite it."

Serpe grinned. His teeth were bright in the midst of his dirty face and the halogen lamps flashed on his spectacles. "So, we can re-enact the Mayan myth of the Flood!" he said with relish.

"I think I have it," I said. Quickly, I explained my plan. We all made the Sign of the Cross, and headed off to our respective stations. I moved off to the right, keeping an eye as I went on Lychfield, who

157

was still barely moving and had not yet reached the archway.

Stalagmites stood in ranks like soldiers before the lock, and I was able to hide behind one that had a thick base. I peeked out. The two Germans on the platform rested their elbows on the railing, talking and keeping a casual eye on the workers below.

Another outboard motor roared into life. I looked over my shoulder, and saw that Wilmer's boat was moving slowly into line behind Lychfield's. Dean had just finished loading the third, and was giving the Ququmatz a few last instructions before boarding.

"Hurry up, Ari," I whispered. "Lychfield is getting away with the Kaiser's gold!"

At that moment, there came a violent hiss, like an angry snake, as Ari's second tear gas canister shattered among the feet of the Ququmatz. A grey cloud expanded among them. They instantly scattered, coughing, spluttering, crying out in fear and pain. Dean threw himself to the floor of the dock.

I reached into my pocket and drew out one of Ari's tiny TNT charges. I turned to face the German sailors before me. They had straightened up in alarm, but at the moment they evidently didn't know what to do. The hand of one hovered over the trigger of the machine gun, but he could see no one to shoot.

A sharp crack rang out, and the sailor staggered backwards, clutching his shoulder. Blood oozed between his fingers. His partner stared down at the reeling Ququmatz, and saw Fritz, half-concealed behind a large rock, his Mauser leveled and aimed with deadly accuracy. He seized the trigger of the machine gun, but Fritz was faster. The Mauser rang out, and the sailor flew backwards, his arms spread wide.

That was my signal. I rose from my hiding place and swung myself up the steel steps.

An explosion shook the cavern, and I snatched a glance towards the boats. Serpe had flung the other TNT charge at Lychfield's boat, but he had mistimed the fuse, and it had exploded about six feet from its target. The force of the explosion blew pieces of gold from the top of the pile into the water. Lychfield and the Germans ducked. Fire raked the deck for an instant. But it did no other damage. Lychfield rose again, his head darting this way and that in search of their assailant. The boat was undamaged.

I lit the fuse of my TNT and slotted it between the top of the lock gate and the roof of the cave. There was only about eight inches of space, beyond which was a small cavern full of hydrogen sulphate.

Then I ran like the clappers.

CHAPTER 13
THE UNDERGROUND RIVER

I sped up towards the ledge where we had entered the cavern. I had set, I thought, a twenty-second fuse for the TNT, and when I had reached eighteen in my head, I lowered myself to the ground, thinking to hide from the blast behind one of the stalagmites. But I must have counted slowly, because the TNT went off before I'd properly taken cover. The blast bowled me over, and I sprawled along the ground. A wave of heat billowed over me, roasting my back for a moment. Briefly, blue light lit everything around me. Then I heard bits of debris pattering on the ground all about me; a few struck me in the back. When I looked back the way I had come, I could see a luminous blue and orange cloud unfurling along the roof of the cavern, engulfing one by one the halogen lamps. The acrid smell of burning wafted out with it.

As I watched, one of the lock gates swung open on its hinge, and water poured from the gap. A mountain of water rolled down the slope towards the dock. It swelled the river, picked up the third boat, raised it high, and tipped it over on its side. For a moment, gold glittered in the air, scintillating through the descending cloud of smoke. Then it was gone.

I looked towards the archway. Lychfield's boat was not in sight. Wilmer's was almost through—I could see the outboard motor just before the water rose all about it; but I couldn't see whether it had been sunk.

My ears still rang with the sound of the explosion. Picking myself up, I shook my head and staggered on. Waiting beside the door by which we had entered the cavern were Ari, Fritz and Serpe, all staring anxiously towards me. Ari broke out into a run and threw her arms about me, planting a huge kiss on my lips.

"Thanks God!" she gulped. "I thought for a moment you weren't going to get up!"

"It wasn't really all that dangerous," I replied; but my knees were shaking.

"The other two boats," insisted Fritz, "*schnell!*"

"Right," I answered; but I hadn't thought out anything past blowing up the lock. I'd hoped the flood would sink all three boats. "How are we going to follow them?" I turned to Serpe. "Do you know where this river comes out?"

Serpe shrugged. "This river, I did not even know it was here," he said. "Perhaps it goes all the way to the sea."

"Then we'll have to swim for it." I peered down at the swollen river below. Water still cascaded into it through the broken lock. Below our feet—not so far below them now—it still churned and seethed like a bag of snakes.

The lights flickered. I looked up at them. Water and fire had damaged the wiring.

"We have to be quick," I said, "or we'll be swimming in total darkness. Are you all ready?" With another Sign of the Cross, we all moved to the brink of the ledge. "All right then, let's go," I said. Fritz dived first; the current swept him away. Serpe followed swiftly. Ari leaped in after Serpe. Then, taking a deep breath, I jumped.

I plunged into a swirling chaos, and was completely disoriented for a few moments; but I've been thrown off boats and submarines so many times, I've sort of worked out what to do. I tried to relax until I could get my bearings. Something hard—a rock— struck me on the shoulder as the eddy threw me against the far side of the river.

I resurfaced and struck out with a cupped hand. I had to fight against the currents, which were trying to spin me round and round. I reached out for something to hold me steady, and gripped a rock. It was slippery, but my fingers held, and I was able to take a look around.

The lights flickered again, but I could see the archway I was aiming for. I couldn't see the others, but I couldn't afford any time to reflect on what their fates might be. I just prayed for their safety, and plunged into the waters once more.

The water was stiller down deep, and I sailed through the blue depths with a kick of the feet. The archway flashed overhead, and I swam higher until my head emerged in the next cavern. I was in a long water-filled passageway with rocky sides. The roof was very close—the taller waves dashed my head against it—and halogen lamps hung from it. They too guttered like old candles. I saw someone else's head before me—Ari's, her long hair streaming out behind her. I swam with the strongest strokes I could muster along the surface to catch up.

The lights above us flickered for the last time and went out. For a moment, we drifted along, carried through utter darkness by the current. But then I began to discern shapes—a shoulder of rock off to my right, a low dip in the roof just ahead—and realized that it was not totally dark. Ahead, I could just make out patches of green light, growing in intensity as we neared them.

Just then, we emerged into a cave as big as a warehouse. The light, I saw, came through ragged gaps in the roof of the cave. It was green because it shone through fern leaves and palm fronds. The cavern was closer to the surface than I had expected.

Water filled most of the cave, but directly ahead of us was a large land-mass. I could see Ari's hands rise rhythmically from the water as she swam for this island. I followed suit, and a moment later was dragging myself onto flat ground covered with underbrush and thick tangles of ferns. Ari lay on her back beside me, her chest heaving with the exertion. I threw myself down beside her, reaching out to take her hand.

"Well, we made it," I said. "Made it somewhere, at least."

"But where are we?" Ari pushed herself up on her elbows. "And where are Fritz and Serpe?"

We both hauled ourselves upright. "I don't see them," I said. "What is that?" A few yards inland was a towering wall. Grass and even flowers sprouted between the great square-hewn stones from which it was constructed. At the top, I could see a statue of some kind.

"Is that statue a bird?" I asked, pointing.

Ari looked up. Her brows knit together. "I think it might be an owl," she said. "That would be bad. Owls were always bad omens in the ancient world. The Mayans certainly didn't like them."

"So, why would they build statues of them?" I wondered.

At that moment, we were interrupted by a voice. A hundred yards off to our left, Serpe and Fritz had clawed their way up onto the island, and were waving for our attention.

"There they are," said Ari with relief, and we trudged off towards them. It wasn't easy going, as

164

the undergrowth was thick. After a while, having recovered from their swim, Fritz and Serpe got to their feet, and we met in the centre of the shore.

"Well, here we are," I said, "wet but safe."

"For the moment, Herr McCracken, for the moment," said Fritz, pulling his Mauser out of his pocket and checking it carefully.

Ari and Serpe were gazing in wonder at the walls we had seen earlier. The Mayans had built what looked like an athletic stadium: a pair of grandstands, with ranked seating, stood on either side of what would originally have been a wide lawn. Now, it was a wilderness of bushes, ferns, and even small trees. Lianas dangled from the ceiling. At the far end of the court stood another building, with seats, but also with a couple of doors and a stone hoop some way off the ground.

"*Signora*," said Serpe, "do you know what this is?"

"I think it's a ball-court," replied Ari. Serpe nodded. "Grandstands for the spectators," Ari went on, "and a locker room right ahead for the players— they got onto the court by those doors." Serpe nodded vigorously in agreement.

"Why are there statues of owls?" I asked, as we walked slowly down the court, the grandstands on either side of us. At each of the corners was a statue of a bird, each of a similar size. One of them, I saw, had only one leg; another had no legs and a skull instead of a head.

"Why the statues of the owls at a ball-court?" said Serpe, the eyes behind those spectacles darting this way and that. "That is a good question." Light dawned on him suddenly, and his eyes widened as he gasped. "Perhaps," he said, "these owls are the messengers of the gods of Xibalba."

"She-bubbly?" I asked.

"Xibalba," Ari corrected me, "the Mayan underworld."

"*Si, appunto, signora,*" replied Serpe. "The gods of Xibalba possessed four owl-messengers: the arrow-owl, who pierced like an arrow; the one-legged owl; the macaw owl, who was red like blood; and the skull owl. The Mayans did not like owls, they hated them. Always, owls were messengers of sickness and death. These four owls, they came to summon Mayan souls to Xibalba." He smiled, understanding at last. "The owls summoned Mayan souls to Xibalba, where they first must play Ollamaliztli, the Mayan ball-game, if they were to earn the right to go on to the afterlife."

"I don't want to go to the afterlife," I said, "not now, anyway. I just want to catch up with Lychfield and his German gold."

We had reached the far end of the ball-court now, and I started climbing the tiers of seating in one of the grandstands. It was steep, and I was panting again by the time I got to the top.

"You know, I don't think this is actually an island," I said. "It's more of a peninsula." The blue waters surrounded the ball-court on three sides in a horseshoe shape, and I paused at the top of the grandstand to show the others what I could see.

Immediately, a gunshot rang out, and I threw myself to the floor. Peering over the top of the grandstand, I saw Wilmer's boat below. A whiff of smoke drifted from the end of his Luger. Seeing me, he loosed off another shot, so that I had to duck again.

"Lychfield?" guessed Ari, who had climbed up just behind me.

"Wilmer," I corrected her. "There's another archway of rock leading out of this cave, and he's in the middle of it."

I had had time to see something else, though, and I told Ari quickly how one of the German sailors had scaled the cliff to the top of the archway. "I have no idea what he was doing," I concluded.

At that moment, the comparative silence of the cavern was shattered by a loud explosion. Smoke belched out from the archway and rose towards the vent overhead. I leaped to my feet and gazed down at the wreckage of the archway. The rubble dislodged by the explosion had completely blocked the archway.

"Well, so much for following Wilmer that way," I said.

"Perhaps there's another way," said Ari.

Serpe was on his feet, scanning the ball-court below with his eyes. "Perhaps there is a concealed way out," he said. "Perhaps the secret is in the Olla-maliztli. The souls of the dead must play Ollamaliz-tli to get from this world to the next, to Xibalba. It was the very first of the tests. The game opened a doorway for them. Perhaps we must play the game and open the door."

"How is it played?" I asked.

"It's a bit like basketball," Ari explained. My look of incomprehension prompted a further defini-tion: "It's a brand-new game, very popular in colleg-es back home. The object is to throw a ball through a hoop." She pointed. "That hoop is different from a basketball hoop—it's on its side, rather than hori-zontal."

"All right," I said, "where can we find a ball?"

"In the myth, Hunahpu was summoned to Xi-balba," said Serpe, searching with his eyes, "and he tied his rubber ball above his house before leaving home." His arm shot out. "There!" Without wait-ing to explain, he dashed off along the top of the grandstand, crossing to the flat top of the locker-room building. We all followed him, but he waved us off. "Go down! Go down!" he shouted. So we did. And when we all stood on the ball-court again, we looked up to see Serpe on top of the locker-room building, his arms wide as if he were walking a tight-rope. When he reached the centre, he paused, stooped, and reached down.

Then we could all see what he had seen: a ball in a net, suspended from the very top of the locker-room building. Serpe's hands worked busily at the net, and with a startling suddenness, the ball came loose. It struck the top tier of the seats up there and bounced in a high arc.

"Catch it!" I said. "Spread out!"

The ball bounced again on a lower tier and described a graceful curve through the air. It sailed high over our heads and plunged into thick vegetation behind Fritz. We all ploughed through the undergrowth to where we had last seen it.

"Here it is, Herr McCracken!" shouted Fritz, and we hurried over to him. The ball was about the size of a European football, and solid rubber.

"Serpe," I said, as he hurried towards us, "how is your plan supposed to work?"

Serpe shrugged. "*Non capisco*," he said, "I do not know. It just . . . how is it in English? . . . it matches the myth, it suits the story."

I gave a big sigh. "Just pray, and play ball," said Ari, kissing me on the nose. "Have faith."

"Right," I said. I took the ball from Fritz and tested its weight—it was nine or ten pounds, I reckoned. I spun on my heel and hurled it at the hoop.

It fell way short. Serpe had it in a moment, and he cast it back at the hoop. It bounced from the rim. Ari picked it up.

"Whew!" she said. "This must have been a tough game—you'd lose points if the ball bounced from the ground more than once."

"Then we've already lost!" I observed.

She tossed the ball, but it fell short. In a few moments, we were panting and giggling, racing to retrieve the ball after it fell, never getting it through the hoop.

"These games," said Serpe breathlessly, "often they would last for several days, and the players would have bruises permanently."

"If they weren't sacrificed," I noted, wiping my brow.

"Even if they were sacrificed," said Serpe. "You have to admit, Cracky—that bruise would be very permanent!"

"But they played in teams, didn't they?" I said. I had found the ball, and hurled it at Serpe, who was closer to the hoop than I. Serpe fended the ball away from his head, then bent over to pull it out of the undergrowth.

"That is very true," he said, "but the teams, they were small—only two or four players. And still it was difficult, *molto difficile*. It is a very small hoop, and a very large ball." He held it in both hands in front of his face, and with a graceful movement, going up on is tiptoes, sent the ball sailing through the air. It rattled around the hoop, but fell out again. I dashed over, snatched it up, and tossed it straight up in the air. Serpe leaped forward and batted it with both hands so that it sailed straight through the hoop, light showing all the way around.

"Bravo!" he cried. "Not basketball—volleyball!"

The ball passed through the hoop cleanly and dropped behind it. We all distinctly heard a click as the ball struck the ground. It wasn't just the ball hitting the ground—something moved, some well-engineered piece, a pressure pad of some kind. With a grinding sound, one of the doors in the centre of the locker-room building opened inwards. Within, all was dark, but daylight fell on the top few steps of a flight of stairs.

"Couldn't we have just stepped on that pressure pad to open the door?" said Ari skeptically.

"It was probably engineered to open on the precise pressure of a precise weight from a precise height and a precise angle," I replied, crowding with the others into the doorway.

"The stairs to Xibalba," said Serpe in wonder.

But my heart began to sink. "What's that noise?" I asked.

"It sounds like a river," said Ari, slipping her hand about my arm. And indeed it did—far below, we could all hear the purling of a river—no doubt the river Lychfield and Wilmer had taken.

"But there is another noise, Frau McCracken," said Fritz, his eyes even wider than usual. "It is like someone crackling greaseproof paper."

Serpe caught his breath. He went down on one knee and peered down the steps into the darkness. I sank down beside him and stared into the pit. As my eyes grew used to it, I thought I could see some kind of movement on the floor. It was as if the whole floor were moving continually. And now we could all hear the rattling noise, like dry leaves rustling, that Fritz had heard.

Serpe turned his face to me. "According to the myth," he said, "after the ball-game is coming the river of scorpions."

CHAPTER 14
INTO XIBALBA

I continued to look through the opening, and now I could see thousands of the tiny monsters, their carapaces clicking and rattling as they clambered over each other. It wasn't so much a river of scorpions as a sea of them, stretching down a rocky slope to the bank of the river. As if in mockery of our hopes, I saw yellow light on the walls—the searchlight of Wilmer's boat, as it drifted into sight below. There was all the Kaiser's gold, and it was separated from us by a sea of venomous arachnids.

"How do they get across the river of scorpions in the myth?" I asked.

Serpe shrugged. "The myth, it just says, 'They passed over the river of scorpions, where there were scorpions beyond counting, but they were not stung.'"

"It must be nice to be a mythic hero," I grunted. Below, Wilmer's boat turned a corner. The light from its searchlight shone on the wall ahead, picking out the boat's outline in silhouette. Then it rounded another corner and was gone. I muttered a curse under my breath.

Serpe took off his spectacles and wiped them on his shirt. Since his shirt was filthy, the action didn't help much, and he frowned before replacing them on his nose and speaking. "During the rituals offered to the gods of death," he said thoughtfully, "young men, to ward off evil, walked across beds of coals, of glowing embers. These embers, it seems to me, they represent the fires of Xibalba—how would you say it?—the punishing fires, the purging fires." He paused. "These scorpions—they fear the fire. They run away from it. This is what the myth and the ritual tell us. If we had some fire," he went on, his eyes narrowed behind his spectacles, "then perhaps we can be making the path through these scorpions."

"Great idea, Serpe," I said. "What do we have that will burn?" Casting around, my eye lighted on the rubber ball. "Great Scott!" I cried. "That's it! Fritz, pass me your Mauser."

Fritz took the beloved pistol from his belt and handed it over. I popped the top round out of the chamber and handed the gun back to Fritz. With Ari's stiletto, I cut through the bullet's casing and poured the gunpowder into a small heap. Then I piled some dry grass over it.

"Serpe," I said, "hand me your spectacles, please."

He pulled them from his nose and, blinking, passed them to me. I glanced up at the light coming through the roof from above, and positioned one lens to catch it. A little dot of white appeared among the grey powder. A moment later, a fizz erupted from it, and flames sprouted among the dry grass. In no time at all, I had fanned the flames into quite a blaze. I returned the spectacles to Serpe.

"This is a great place to start a fire," I said. "No breeze." I held out my hand towards Fritz. "Would you pass me the rubber ball, please, Fritz?" I placed it so that the flames from the burgeoning fire touched its side. Before too long, the rubber caught light, churning out clouds of oily black smoke. "Get ready, everybody!" I said, and shoved the ball into the opening.

The fireball bounced over the steps, for a second illuminating the mass of terrible arachnids in the chamber beyond. Then it landed among them, scattering them left and right. They scuttled away from its flaming path.

"Quickly!" I shouted, and the others dashed down the slope after the fireball. I took up the rear.

The ball left a stream of fire behind it, as pieces of rubber stuck to the ground and remained behind, spouting flame. It looked like a comet as it rolled and bounced along towards the river. The orange light showed the scorpions scrabbling away in fear, and lit up the roof above us, which was a lot closer than I would have guessed. The ball pumped out lots of black smoke, which got into our eyes and throats, choking us and smarting. We ran on down the slope, hardly able to check our course.

The fireball bounced one last time and dropped, hissing, into the river. We all followed, our arms flailing. We had built up momentum chasing the fireball, and could not stop. Four splashes, a kick of the heels, and we were on the opposite bank of the river, safe from the nightmare of stingers and pincers. We got dripping to our feet, and found we stood on a narrow shelf of rock that followed the course of the river like a footpath beside a canal.

"Look!" I said, pointing. We seemed to be at the entrance to another natural tunnel, into which the river ran. It was lit by more vents in the roof, but far off along it was a yellow light—Wilmer's boat. "We're not even far behind," I grinned. We took off after Wilmer, but couldn't go fast—we had run and jumped and swum continually for I couldn't tell how long, and were beginning to be worn out. Ari lagged far behind, and I dropped back to trot beside her.

"Are you all right?" I asked.

"I'm a little spent, that's all," she replied. "I'll be fine."

"Serpe!" I called. "What's next, according to the myth?"

Serpe looked back as he walked. "What is next, Cracky? It is a river of blood, and—and then, another river."

"Of what?" I asked. "Spiders? Beer? Mousetraps?"

"No, none of those," replied Serpe. "As a matter of fact, it is a river of . . . I cannot tell what it is in English. *Liquame.*"

"Pus!" said Ari, her nose wrinkling. "A river of pus!"

"No wonder I hadn't thought of that," I remarked. We were in the next tunnel now, and our way was lit from above, but the path did not run straight—stalagmites blocked our path, or rocky protrusions, and we had to slow down to pick or squeeze our way around them. Sometimes, our path would drop dramatically, and we'd have to walk through water. "We'll never catch them at this pace!" I lamented bitterly.

"We can't go much faster than this," panted Ari. She came to a halt, bent over, and braced herself against her knees.

"Ari—" I started, slowing and turning.

She held up a hand. "I just can't go as fast as you can," she said, gasping for breath, "at least, not right now. You go on."

I paused, suspended between my expectant wife and the Kaiser's gold, like a magnet between two positive poles.

"Cracky!" came Serpe's voice. "Please, make haste!"

"I'll be with you in a moment!" I called back.

"You ought to go on," said Ari. "I'll catch up with you as soon as I can."

"You'll do nothing of the sort," I said. I stooped down in front of her. "Climb on my back," I said. "I'll carry you *and* the baby!"

"But the gold," said Ari. "Think of the War. Think what will happen if the Kaiser gets all that gold!"

I gave a snort. "I can't imagine what we're fighting for at all," I said, "if we can't even help our own families. Get on my back, and don't argue any more about it."

She put her arms around my neck, and I held her under her knees. She was surprisingly light—it was hard to believe the baby was there. But I certainly couldn't move fast. The ground seemed to become more uneven. It was tricky to manoeuvre, even with the light coming from above.

The path ran out just ahead of us. A rope bridge spanned the river, and the path continued along the further bank.

"Can you walk across the bridge?" I asked.

"Of course I can!" replied Ari, climbing down. "It'll be just like Thera."

"I hope not," I answered. "The bridge in Thera broke when you were on it."

"Then I'll go first," said Ari, striding out along the bridge. After a few paces, she said, "The rope doesn't seem old."

"It couldn't be Mayan," I replied. "Rope couldn't survive for a thousand years. Lychfield probably built this."

We had barely gained the further bank, when we saw something move in the shadows ahead, and Fritz's voice came to us: "Herr McCracken, come quickly— found we have the river of blood!"

Ari and I exchanged glances. "Really?" I said. "It's really blood?"

Fritz spread his hands. "It is not I would know, Herr McCracken," he said. "The water, it is red like blood."

"Can you manage?" I asked, turning to Ari.

"I'll be fine," she said, waving me on. "I'll just be a little behind you, that's all."

I shook my head. "I'll keep pace with you," I said, determined; and to my surprise she didn't argue with me at all.

We went on through the underground passage, Fritz almost dancing with impatience.

"I think I hear running water," said Ari.

She was right—just behind the sound of the river was another, more urgent sound of water cascading from a height. We quickened our pace, and soon found ourselves in another cavern. The river emerged from our tunnel into the cavern, and wound through its length.

"*Schauen Sie mal her, Herr McCracken,*" said Fritz, so excited now that he forgot to speak English, "*der Fluss von Blut!*"

Through one of the vents in the roof came a cascade of water, as red as blood. Downstream of the waterfall, the river itself was a deep crimson in colour. Serpe sat on a small rocky prominence overlooking the little pool into which the "blood" spilled.

"So, how did those Mayan heroes get across the river of blood?" I asked Serpe.

Serpe looked round at me. "The river of blood!" he announced. "I did not think I would ever see it, but here it is! How did the Mayan heroes get across it? The myth, it says that they were able to cross over the river because they did not drink from it."

"Anyone who drank from the river would know it wasn't really blood," I pointed out. "But what is it?" I stooped, dipped my finger into the crimson water, and touched it to the end of my tongue. I could faintly taste something—a bit like raspberries or blackberries, but with something else too—dark chocolate, perhaps. "Well, it's not blood," I said. "I think they just invented the myth to prevent everyone from drinking from this river. It's too good to share! Greedy blokes, these Mayans—it's delicious." I looked up the waterfall at the palm trees that bowed their heads over it. "What kind of trees are those?" I asked. "Do they have fruit of any kind?"

"Those trees," said Serpe, "are acai palms. The natives call them *iwacai*."

"Ha!" cried Fritz. "This I know." He bent down beside me, scooped up a handful of water in his hands, and drank deeply. "*Jawohl!*" he concluded. "I am speaking with many of the Ququmatz about food, and this I have tasted before—the berries of the *iwacai* palm! It is very delicious."

"So much for the river of blood," I said, and we all drank deeply from the pool. "I hope the other river is equally innocent!"

"*Guarda!*" cried Serpe. We all followed his gaze up the waterfall to the irregular circle of sky at the top. "Did you see the bird? The bird with the long tail, the forked tail? This they call in these parts the boatswain's bird—never do they fly inland. We must be close to the sea now."

I looked at the vent above us. It didn't look like a difficult climb. I said, "You all go on; I'll catch you up. I want to see what's going on, if I can."

As they continued the journey, I grasped a liana, planted my boots firmly against the rock beside the waterfall, and hauled myself up. Spray from the waterfall misted me continually, and my foot slipped on the wet rocks more than once, but inch by inch I climbed to the vent. Once there, it was relatively easy to scramble up onto firm ground.

Straightening, I found myself among the acai palms we had seen from below. Inland, the ground rose sharply, and the river that formed the waterfall tumbled down between shining rocks into the vent. A salty scent hung on the air, and I could see a glimmer of blue between the trees. A couple of paces took me to the edge of the palms. I took out Rob Roy's dirk and cleared some of the undergrowth away.

Before me was a miniature forest, no more than knee-height. It was composed of shrubs with large, round leaves, which I learned later were called seagrape, and a kind of scrambling undergrowth, like a thick mat of green, called sea purslane. A few bare grey trees sprouted here and there. The ground dropped below my feet to sand-dunes and the white stripe of a beach, with the shimmering blue of the sea beyond it.

And on the sea was the narrow body of a submarine, its conning tower, rising like the dorsal fin of a shark, emblazoned with the call-signal U-53.

CHAPTER 15
ANOTHER DANGEROUS PURSUIT

I scrambled back down the liana and into the cave of the river of blood. I had to swim a red lake to catch up with the others. They had paused to wait for me, crouching behind some rock formations. Beyond the rock formations, I could see the steep sides of cliffs. The open sky was above us.

"What did you find?" asked Ari in a whisper.

"Not much," I replied, "just a U-boat. What about you?"

"Not much," answered Ari, "just a river of pus."

"You always find the nicest things," I said.

"It's really just calcium deposits," explained Ari. "The calcium makes the water look white."

"So it's calcium, is it?" I raised my eyebrows. "I see being married to me is beginning to benefit you." I rose a little to peek over the top of the rock. The water below us, fed by another waterfall, gentler this time, was white as milk. What really commanded my attention, however, was that Lychfield's boat was framed by the jagged, nearly vertical sides of the cliff. Through the opening, and beyond Lychfield's boat, I knew the U-53 rested at anchor.

"More locks, Cracky," said Serpe, pointing directly below us. The crimson water, I saw, flowed into the top lock in a system of three that would take any vessel gently down to the level of the creamy pool below it.

"Why a river of pus?" I mused. "Why not a river of milk? I mean, it's neither of those things really, but why even think of a river of pus and a river of blood?"

Serpe shrugged. "Why blood and pus?" he said. "That is the Mayans, you know. It was—how would you say?—a very brutal culture. Their gods demanded the sacrifices, all the time. Always, they were thinking of blood and pus, I think."

I sighed. "I suppose we'll have to go after that treasure," I said. "Fritz, do you have a clear shot at Lychfield?"

"*Nein*, Herr McCracken," replied Fritz, shaking his head. "Out of range he is. But I could get those sailors with Herr Wilmer."

"Just to wound," Ari reminded him.

I nodded. "Let's give it a *shot*," I suggested.

"Better than just *barreling* on through," responded Ari with a half-smile.

"*Shell* we start?" I countered. It was a poor pun, but I didn't have time to think of anything better.

Fritz managed it, though. "It has be*gun*," he said, shouldering his way between us and thumbing off the safety catch of the Mauser.

"Ari, can you and Serpe get down to the beach level that way?" I asked. There were steps off to the left. "Fritz and I will climb down the locks. We'll out-flank them. When Fritz opens fire, they'll be focusing on us, and you can get down safely."

"God be with you," said Ari, with a quick kiss. Turning, she dashed away with Serpe.

"And with you," I responded, pausing a moment before redirecting my attention to Wilmer. Neither he nor the German sailors had spotted us yet.

Fritz closed one of his eyes, sighted along the barrel of the Mauser, and gently squeezed the trigger. The gun kicked a little in his hand as the shot echoed about the stone walls. One of the German sailors leaped backwards and spiraled, his arms wide like a strange windmill, from the boat and into the water.

The other two looked around in alarm, and picked us out almost at once. Whipping out their Lugers, they fired off a series of rapid shots. Fritz and I ducked a moment, but when the firing slackened, Fritz popped up again and loosed off another round.

"*Ach, Gott im Himmel!*" he said roughly. "I miss—but the other *Seeman* is gone. There is only Wilmer in the boat now."

"Where could he have gone?" I asked.

"I did not see, Herr McCracken," replied Fritz.

"Well, there's nothing for it, now," I said. "Are you ready?"

"*Jawohl*, Herr McCracken," replied Fritz.

185

We both sprang upright, vaulted over the rocks that screened us from the boat, and jumped. Wilmer fired twice while we were in the air, but the bullets sang over our heads and thudded into the rock. We hit the water of the first lock with a splash, and kicked to the wooden gates opposite.

Just one more lock to go, and then we'd be able to get at Wilmer's boat. Once again, I was breathing heavily, and I wondered with a flutter in my stomach what Ari was doing.

I peered over the top of the wooden gate, but ducked immediately, as Wilmer saw me and fired off his Luger at my head.

"*Zehn*," said Fritz. "Herr Wilmer has all his bullets used, Herr McCracken. We go now, *ja*?"

"Right, on three, we'll go over the top," I said. "Ready? One, two, three—go!" And we both leaped over the lock gate.

This time we landed in soft mud and had to roll. Another two shots rang out, kicking out chunks of the lock gate behind us.

"Wilmer must have reloaded," I said.

"Not Wilmer," said Fritz, his voice raspy with the effort. "Wrong direction."

We scrambled towards the boat, our feet sliding in the mud. But we reached the shadow of the boat's stern safely.

I heard soft laughter from the bows, and then came Wilmer's voice: "Okay, McCracken, why don't you just stand up and see what the tactical situation is?" Puzzled, I rose from our cover and gazed along the length of the hull. As I rose, the piles of treasure seemed to drop and reveal three figures at the far end of the raft. The German sailor was back, and had brought Ari with him. Wilmer held her firmly in front of him. The Luger's barrel was pressed firmly against the side of her head.

My blood began to boil—I could feel it coursing through my veins. Any moment now, if no one restrained me, I felt I would leap on Wilmer and tear him to shreds. I pulled myself up onto the boat and began to advance dangerously on him and the German sailor. Fritz came behind me.

"Oh, don't get any ideas, Mr. McCracken," said Wilmer. "I know you're pretty quick, but my trigger finger is quicker."

"Are you all right, love?" I asked.

"So far," said Ari. She didn't dare move her head in a nod. But then, quite distinctly, she gave me a slow wink. I'd seen that wink once before, I recalled, on Pier 54 in New York Harbour.

"What have you done with Serpe?" I demanded.

"Oh, he's not dead," replied Wilmer, "or not yet, anyway. But he's going to be asleep for a while. Dieter here is trained in unarmed combat. But I think you've got other fish to fry right now. Your wife's safety, for example."

"You wouldn't be such a monster, Wilmer," I said. "She's expecting a baby—why don't you take me as a hostage instead?" I edged a tiny bit closer—tiny enough not to be noticed.

"Expecting a baby?" repeated Wilmer. "Lucky you, old sport! I'd congratulate you, but—well, I suppose I ought to warn you as well. Shooting two McCrackens at once seems like a pretty good economy to me. So just don't move any closer."

"I'm not moving," I said through clenched teeth.

"That goes for you too, Mr. Bauer," said Wilmer. "Put down that antiquated pistol of yours, or I'll fire. I have plenty of bullets left."

"*Fünf,*" said Fritz, almost spitting the word as he placed his Mauser on top of a statue of a jaguar. He held his hands out so Wilmer would see they were nowhere near the sidearm.

"What I need you to do," said Wilmer, "is climb out of this boat and stay here so we can proceed to the U-boat. I'll release your wife once we get there safely. Can you swim, Ari? It's okay to call you Ari, isn't it?" he asked with a smile.

"I can swim," Ari confirmed.

"Good. Dieter." Wilmer turned his head slightly to address the German sailor. "Go and open the lock gate."

Dieter snapped his heels and turned to leave.

But in that moment, Wilmer's attention had been divided. Ari winked again, but not at me this time. On her signal, Fritz lunged for his Mauser. At the same time, Ari pretended to faint, just as she had on Pier 54. Wilmer found himself dragged down by her weight, and he let her go. She rolled away to starboard. Wilmer's Luger swept round at Fritz, who had not yet had time to aim. His finger reflexively pulled on the trigger.

"No!" I shouted, and leaped forward.

A pistol shot crashed out. Against my expectations, it wasn't Fritz who fell; it was Wilmer who flew backwards against the gunwale of the boat. Dieter, half out of the boat, reached for his own sidearm, but another shot sent him flying out of the boat and into the water, which did not turn crimson all around him, as it was already crimson.

Ari was curled up on the deck. I scooped her up and held her close to me, kissing her over and over again. She opened her eyes and kissed me back.

"I think we're going to have to rehearse that whole me-being-held-at-gunpoint scenario some more," she said. "I need a few different escape plans."

"Why mess with something that works perfectly well every time?" I answered.

"Why didn't Wilmer fire?" Ari asked.

A roar of anguish came from Wilmer, and we both looked over at him. He was slouched against the gunwale, clutching his shoulder. Blood ran between his fingers.

"He did not fire, Frau McCracken," said Fritz, the Mauser still smoking in his hand, "because the Luger, it jammed. It is the design flaw with them."

"Ari, will you go and find Serpe, please?" I said. "And, Fritz—please open the lock gate. We can't let Lychfield escape with that gold. I'll find a rope and tie Wilmer up."

Wilmer started muttering with impotent fury at this, and there was something odd about his tone of voice—I realized that he was slipping in and out of consciousness, probably from the shock. Meanwhile, I could feel the boat begin to rise as Fritz let water into the lower lock.

"Herr McCracken," called Fritz at last, "the lock is open!"

I eased up on the throttle and nudged the nose of the boat out through the open gate. Fritz jumped down lightly from the winch as I passed; a moment later, Ari joined us with a dazed Serpe, who was rubbing his head as he came. She went instantly over to Wilmer to bind his wound.

Our stern cleared the lock. Ahead of us lay clear water, all the way to the ragged hole to the outside world. I opened up the throttle, and the boat jumped forward. Fritz was caught off balance, and rocked a little. I turned the bows a little, hoping there were no submerged rocks in our way. We were in too much of a hurry to worry about that; Lychfield already had a clear lead on us.

The cliffs on either side closed in. Shadows covered our little boat. Then sunlight flashed over us, and the bows bounced as a wave hit them. We were in the open, the cave lying further and further astern.

Ahead of us lay U-53. Lychfield's raft was already alongside the submarine, tethered to it by a lengthy rope. The captain was climbing up the conning tower, where another couple of officers awaited him. Fritz leveled his Mauser at the distant scene, but our bows rose and fell with the waves, and he could not aim properly. He and Ari stood side-by-side in the bows, while I manned the motor in the stern. Serpe, swaying with the motion of the sea, had made his way back to join me.

"If I may be allowed a quotation from a famous poet," he said, "though not, I think, so great as Alighieri, on the sudden a Roman thought hath struck me." He pointed to Lychfield's boat. "Perhaps the quickest way of dealing with Professore Liccifieltro is to increase our velocity to ramming speed?"

"We'd dash ourselves against the submarine," I said. "That would destroy both vessels."

"*Si, appunto*," replied Serpe. "We must, of course, jump clear before the impact."

I had only the briefest moment to consider Serpe's suggestion. "Tell the others," I concluded, and Serpe moved forward.

A few sailors had emerged from the conning tower and were approaching Lychfield, who had remained in the boat. He was stacking the gold along the side of the U-boat. We were about a quarter of a mile away, and I could hear the boots on the metal ladders. I adjusted the rudder. The nose of the boat pointed directly amidships of Lychfield's boat. We sped across the waves towards our target, like a rocket.

At that moment, the German captain saw our approach. He stared for a moment, confused. Then he leaned over the conning tower and shouted some instructions. The sailors below, who had been running to help Lychfield with the gold, doubled back on themselves and dashed for the deck-gun.

Lychfield turned and shielded his eyes from the sunlight with his hand. He took out his Luger and fired a series of shots, hardly aiming at all. Ari, Fritz and Serpe ducked. Most of the shots went wide. One bullet smacked into the golden statue of a god, which whirled into the sea.

The deck-gun turned its yawning muzzle on us. One of the sailors slotted a shell into the chamber and stepped back. I could see the other tug on the firing pin. A flash of light and smoke obscured the gun for a moment. There's always a moment's delay between the report of a large-calibre gunshot and the impact of the shell, and if you're being fired at, that interval seems to last infinitely. But you're frozen—

you can't do anything. All I could do was keep my hand on the outboard motor and pray. It felt as if I could pray a whole rosary, a whole novena. All I could actually do was begin a Hail Mary. Without thinking, I ducked as the shell screamed overhead. It crashed into the sea, sending up a plume of water, about a hundred yards astern.

The sailor at the deck gun began cranking away at the elevator wheel. The muzzle swung downwards. They had gauged their distance, and would not miss again.

The sound of a large gun boomed out across the water.

My first response was confusion. They hadn't had time to reload yet; and the sound seemed to come from a greater distance away than the U-boat; and it was a much smaller calibre than U-53's deck gun. There had been no muzzle flash, no smoke.

A second later, the deck gun dissolved in a plume of golden fire and smoke. The German captain wheeled around, turning the back of his head to us. "*Untertauschen! Untertauschen!*" The yell came to us clear across the water. Then he vanished from the conning tower. The U-boat began to move.

"He's diving," I said, under my breath. The undertow would drag us under, I knew. I pulled hard around on the rudder, and the boat turned her nose sluggishly away from our target.

The U-boat's engines churned up a wake behind her. The rope mooring Lychfield's boat to U-53 tautened with a snap, and Lychfield tumbled backwards as his boat was dragged along behind the submarine. Then the U-boat began to drop down in the water. Lychfield picked himself up—even at this distance, I could see that he had begun to panic—and scrambled for the line that secured him to the diving submarine.

Only the conning tower was now above the water. It sent a huge bow-wave up into the air, and much of this water crashed down on Lychfield and his boat. I could see his fingers slipping on the line.

Mysteriously, another shot rang out, and landed far away from us. Another ship, I concluded, must be firing on the U-boat. Coast-guard, perhaps? Royal Navy?

The U-boat slid under the waves. It frothed up the sea all around it into a maelstrom of foam. The stern of Lychfield's boat tipped up into the air. Lychfield and a cloud of glittering Mayan gold hung in the air for a fragment of a second; then the eastern sea swallowed it all up.

Beyond the wreckage, we could see our new ally, sporting the ensign of neither the Mexican Coast Guard nor of the Royal Navy, but the Jolly Roger.

"*Me gusta!*" came the cry of her captain, as the slim prow of the *Fortuna de las Serpientes* bore down

upon the timbers and debris that were the only remnant of the Kaiser's gold.

CHAPTER 16
AN AGRICULTURAL SOLUTION

The *Fortuna*'s engines slowed and she coasted to a halt amid the wreckage of Lychfield's boat. The cable rattled and the anchor gave a splash. Gusta stood in the bows, yelling delightedly and gesticulating.

Serpe cleared his throat. "Ahem, *signori, signora*, when you were descending into the mines to find me, do you remember reading a curse on the wall of one of the chambers?"

Ari paled. "That the eastern sea would swallow anyone who removed the treasure?"

"*Si, appunto.*" I leaned over the gunwale, my eyes scanning the waters. The boat's timbers bobbed up and down on the waves. I had raised the outboard motor, and we barely moved, except with the swell of the ocean. "I am thinking," said Serpe cautiously, "that perhaps we should pray for Professore Oliviero, no?"

"I think that's a wonderful idea," responded Ari. We all made the Sign of the Cross and prayed a Hail Mary, our eyes darting this way and that over the impossibly blue waters of the Gulf of Mexico. Wilmer muttered imprecations at us about superstitions. I prayed for him too.

"There!" shouted Ari, pointing, and I saw what we had been looking for: clinging to a broken timber that rode the waves as they rolled under him was Lychfield, his hair and beard slick with seawater. I breathed a sigh of relief. For a moment, I had thought he had been sucked underwater by the submarine's propellers, but here he was, unhappy but alive. With a prayer of thanks, I lowered the motor into the water again, nudged the tiller, and in a few moments, Fritz and Serpe were reaching down to haul Lychfield into our boat. He lay in a miserable pile beside Wilmer, coughing and spluttering.

At length, he raised his eyes with a baleful glance about the boat. "I suppose you'll be keeping all this gold I mined by my own effort?" he asked with a sneer.

"We'll find something better to do with it than give it to the Kaiser," I replied, turning the boat back towards the *Fortuna*.

Lychfield turned his misery upon Wilmer now. "You fool," he said bitterly, "why did you let them take your boat?"

Wilmer, who had been lamenting his wound, looked up at his former boss. "If you hadn't raced through those tunnels so fast," he said, "we could have fought off that snot-nosed engineer between us. You never want to cooperate—you always want the glory for yourself."

Lychfield found some energy, and threw himself at Wilmer, his fingers scrabbling for his throat. Serpe grabbed Lychfield and heaved him across the narrow deck, away from Wilmer. Wilmer scrambled painfully away from Lychfield.

"If you hadn't gone so slowly," said Lychfield, "we'd be on our way to Germany by now."

Wilmer turned to Serpe, and then to me. "It's all his fault anyway," he complained. "It wasn't really my idea at all. I just wanted to bring all the gold back to the States and put it in a museum. It was Lychfield who wanted to give it to the Germans."

And so the dreary recriminations went monotonously on as our boat came alongside of the *Fortuna*. While I fastened the cable fore and aft, some of Gusta's men scrambled down the ladder to secure Lychfield and Wilmer and to propel them off to the brig.

"Hey, McCracken!" called Gusta, from the deck above us. "That is a lot of gold you have there—do you have a home for it?"

"If I gave it to you," I shouted back, "you'd just lose it!"

Gusta laughed heartily. "Come aboard, *mi amigo!*" he shouted.

Grinning, I followed Ari and Serpe up to the deck, where we were each received into a massive bear-hug from Gusta. Something rough rubbed against my hand, and I looked down to see that Tigre was licking it.

"Señora McCracken," said Gusta, kissing Ari's hand, "your beauty is a delight to me! Welcome aboard the *Fortuna de las Serpientes.*" Turning to Serpe, he said, "I am very glad to meet you, *señor.* Welcome aboard."

"The name of your ship," said Serpe, "the luck of the snakes? I am myself called Campo di Serpenti—the field of snakes."

Gusta raised an eyebrow. "Perhaps," he said, "this is an omen—perhaps you should join us on the *Fortuna.* The life of the pirate might suit you, eh?"

"The life of the pirate?" Serpe shrugged. "Perhaps. But first, I must return to my Maria—she perhaps thinks I am dead. I will have to inform her to the contrary, *signor.*"

Gusta summoned a few sailors and gave them orders to see quarters made available for us, others to bring up the Mayan gold and store it in the hold. As it was carried up the ladder bit by bit, he watched with a bright eye.

"Well, *mi amigo,*" he said, "if you need some suggestions about how you might spend all that gold, let me know." He struck a match and lit a cigar.

The thought came to me of a coffee plantation in Colombia. I saw in my mind's eye the verdant slopes of the Andes, the coffee pickers in wide straw hats moving slowly along the groves, while Gusta surveyed them from his veranda, a cigar between his lips and a pretty dark-haired wife on his knee, while a dozen dark-skinned ragamuffins charged about his feet, brandishing wooden cutlasses and toy flintlocks. It did indeed seem like a good use for the gold, but I would have to talk to Ari before making any promises.

We sailed south. I had to deposit Lychfield and Wilmer with the appropriate authorities, and because of the Revolution, there was neither a British nor an American embassy in Mexico. The nearest friendly port was Belize City, in British Honduras, and Gusta accordingly set sail on that heading. It took us a couple of days to round the Yucatan Peninsula, but then we made our way through the scattered archipelago, and saw the city spread out before us. It was really spread out—in a leisurely fashion, the white-roofed houses were interspersed with palm trees. We moored some distance from the dock, and rowed ashore in the jolly boat.

Government House was a two-story building, white with green shutters and a long staircase leading to the front doors, where a pair of soldiers in tropical khakis stood to attention. One of them, seeing us, sent for his sergeant, who appeared, red-faced and moustachioed, a baton under his arm and a peaked cap crammed on his head, a few moments later.

We explained our purpose, pointing from time to time to our sullen prisoners. At length, the sergeant raised his eyebrows, gave a couple of orders and invited us inside. One of the guards took charge of Lychfield and Wilmer.

The interior of Government House reminded me of a scene from a Jane Austen novel, except that the chairs along the walls were white wicker, and fans revolved lazily from the coffered ceiling. Everything was painted white, except for the floor, which was chequered white and black. Windows in the south wall looked out across a neat lawn to the deep blue of the sea and the paler cloudless blue of the sky. Ari, Serpe and I gazed out at the tropical paradise until the sergeant's voice from behind summoned us.

"The Governor would like to see you," he said, "if you don't mind."

We followed him up a wide flight of stairs, then along a wood-floored landing until we came to a door at the front of the house, which led into the Governor's office.

The Governor stood behind a polished desk, framed by a window that looked out over a lawn with palm trees. "Mr. McCracken, Mrs. McCracken, Mr. Campo di . . . Serpents, how very, very good to see you all. Wilfred Collett, Governor of British Honduras."

We all shook hands, and Collett offered us drinks. I took a gin and tonic.

Collett invited us all to sit in wicker chairs around the unlit and rather unnecessary fireplace.

"Well now," he said, "you've done king and country a service today, and no doubt." We all thanked him, but I squirmed a little. I had expected to drop off the malefactors and then depart. I had no idea why we were still here. Collett went on, "To have frustrated the Kaiser's little scheme was an act of great patriotism, great patriotism indeed, as well as courage." He hesitated. "Is there any of the gold left?"

I thought again of Gusta's coffee plantation in the Andes, of tiny feet pattering around a veranda in numerous games of pirates. I couldn't give the gold both to Gusta and to His Majesty's Government.

Then I remembered Dean's capsized treasure-boat, and I had an inspiration. Perhaps I could give the gold to them both!

"There's quite a lot of gold left in the cave; I'm sure divers could retrieve it," I said.

"Jolly good," replied Collett. "It's not only the Kaiser who needs gold to run the War. Still, the information you've brought will be very useful."

"I'm glad to hear that," I replied casually.

"Oh, to be sure, to be sure," replied the Governor. "His Majesty's Government has been trying to find some means to bring the Americans into the War on our side. We had hoped the sinking of the *Lusitania* would do it, but even that doesn't seem to have been enough. But if President Wilson knew that the Germans were trying to influence the Mexican Revolution, that would make the European War a matter of national security for the Government of the United States. So this whole matter has been very important to us politically, not just economically. Well done, McCracken, well done indeed. This Professor Lychfield will have to be tried in London, of course, and Mr. Wilmer will be turned over to Mr. Ewing, the American Envoy."

I finished my gin and tonic, and set my glass down. "Is there anything else, Governor?" I asked.

"No, nothing at all, just the thanks of His Majesty's Government," replied Collett as we all rose from the chairs. We turned to go, and were almost at the door when Collett added, "But. . . well, actually, there is just one thing more, as a matter of fact, Mr. McCracken." We all turned to face him, and he came forward from the wicker chairs. Most of his gin and tonic remained in his glass, and he swirled it around a little so the ice clinked gently. "You're free to go wherever you wish, of course," he said. "You're a subject of His Majesty, and so free to go anywhere. But if, as a favour to me, you would stay here for a few weeks, at our expense, I would be very grateful."

"Why?" I asked.

Collett took a sip of his drink. "It's just—what do the Americans say?—just a hunch, Mr. McCracken. Something I saw in the diplomatic bag from West Africa. But it's just possible that a man of your talents might be very useful to His Majesty's Government. Give me a chance to cable London. I can let you know in a few days."

"Thank you," I said, and we left.

Serpe went to cable his wife and arrange for a passage back to Italy; we took a cab to Holy Redeemer Cathedral, which was on the waterfront but across the city about half a mile. It was an impressive, whitewashed building, the entrance flanked by a pair of square towers in the Spanish style. We went in, genuflected, and gave thanks for our safety. After a while, I sidled closer to Ari and said, "Isn't this where we were supposed to meet him?"

Ari nodded. "This is the place," she whispered.

Gusta had cabled his brother, Fr. Sarín, and arranged to meet him at this place and hour. But there was no sign of either of them.

We waited and prayed a little more. People began to turn up and fill the pews. We actually attended Mass. At the end of it, Gusta had not showed up. We genuflected once more, and headed for the exit.

As we did so, the doors of the confessional opened, and Gusta and Fr. Sarín emerged. Fr. Sarín was laughing; Gusta's face was dark. They spoke briefly in Spanish before Gusta came over to join us. He dropped to his knee, made the Sign of the Cross, and accompanied us out into the bright sunlight.

"What a question for a brother to ask!" he exploded, once we were in the street. "Of course I have remembered all my sins—in four hours, Judas himself could have remembered all his sins!"

"Four hours?" I said in disbelief.

Gusta took out a watch. "Well, maybe just three hours and forty-five minutes," he said. "Can you believe it—my own brother! Well, I did what I could to persuade Sarín to go into a respectable career, like the Revolution, but he would insist on entering the Church." He shook his head as we crossed the road to look out at the *Fortuna*, riding at anchor across the calm blue waters. "He has always been the black sheep of the family, I suppose. But can you believe the penance he has set me?" We shook our heads. "I am not only to employ my crew on my plantation, but also house any refugees from the Revolution he may send me. My own brother!"

I grinned. "In that case," I said, "the gold is yours."

"You are a good man, *mi amigo*," said Gusta. "And you are a very good woman, *señora*. You are sure you do not want any of the gold yourselves?"

"We have no need of it," answered Ari.

Gusta folded each of us into another embrace. "I have a new brother, and a new sister," he said, "and they are called McCracken." He breathed a deep sigh. "Well, *mis amigos*, I must return to the *Fortuna*, and share the news with my crew. Will you come with me? Sarín will join us for supper this evening, and your man Fritz is cooking—ayiee, *me gusta!*"

"We'll follow in a little while," said Ari.

"*Adios*, then, until later," said Gusta; but turning to leave, he paused a moment and looked at each of us with a twinkling eye. "Well," he said, gripping another cigar between his teeth, "what did I tell you about Professor Lychfield? Did I not tell you that there was something suspicious about all those goings-on in Xulamqamtun? From now on, listen to your good *hermano* Gusta, *si*?" With a final salute, he spun about and swaggered off down the wharf. A few minutes later, we could see the jolly boat returning across the still waters.

"There's an awful lot of gold on that little ship," I said.

"You don't regret giving it to Gusta, do you?" asked Ari.

"Of course not," I replied at once. "No, I have no regrets about this little adventure, except . . . "

"What?"

"Well, it's just still hard to believe that my old college professor turned out to be a traitor, that's all. It's as if the most dependable thing in the world turned out to be a fake."

Some way off along the wharf, we heard the sound of music—a guitar, drums, and an accordion. We listened to it for a few moments, then Ari said,

"Perhaps the problem is trying to find dependability in mere people. Only God is truly dependable."

I nodded slowly. "Nothing's made that more obvious than what's happened in Shoolie-koolie-town."

"Xulamqamtun," Ari corrected me. "And yes, it's very important to see the truth, however unpleasant that is."

"Well, facing truth is something Lychfield and Wilmer have to do now. For years, they've been congratulating each other on how cleverly they've been fooling people."

"They can't fool anyone any more," replied Ari, "not even themselves."

The silence lengthened between us. The music paused, and then struck up a new tune. Ari turned towards the sound. "That's a street café," she said. "Do you think they serve fruit? I have a craving for citrus."

I laughed. "Whatever the two of you prefer!" I said, and we started walking. "So, what's next?" I asked. "Do we go back to New York, or to Europe?"

Ari drew in a deep breath before replying. "I suppose that depends on what Mr. Collett wants with you," she said, "though New York is by far a safer place to have a baby right now than Europe."

"When did McCrackens ever consider their safety first?" I said. "Still, maybe this is the time to play

it safe. And perhaps the War will be over soon, anyway. I hear the Kaiser is short of cash."

"Well, we don't have to decide now," said Ari,
kissing me on the nose. We paused at the little café
and listened for a moment to the music. "Come on,"
she said, "I'll buy you a refresco."

THE END

Panuchos

Ingredients

1 tsp annatto seeds	Juice of 2 lemons
¼ tsp cumin seeds	5 green onions
½ tbsp black pepper-corns	½ cup bitter orange juice
2 whole allspice berries	Vegetable oil
¼ tsp whole cloves	2 lb chicken
¼ cup orange juice	1 can (15 oz) black beans
3 tbsp white vinegar	1 yellow onion
3 cloves garlic	15 soft tortillas
Salt	Lettuce, shredded
2 large anaheim peppers	2 plum tomatoes

Directions

For the xnipec

1. Finely dice the green onions and pour the bitter orange juice over them.

2. Roast one pepper until the skin becomes charred. Making sure to protect your hands, peel the skin off, scrape out the seeds, and slice it finely. Add it to the green onion mixture. Sprinkle salt on it. Set aside to marinade for an hour.

For the achiote paste

1. Grind the annatto seeds, cumin seeds, pepper-corns, allspice berries and cloves together. Slice the other pepper.

2. In a blender or food processor, add the ground spices, orange juice, 2 tbsp vinegar, 2 garlic cloves and 1 tbsp salt to the sliced pepper. Blend until smooth, then add the lemon juice. Set aside.

For the panuchos

1. In a medium bowl, combine 1 tbsp. white vine-gar, the achiote paste, vegetable oil, ¼ tsp salt. Add chicken and turn to coat it well.

2. Fry the chicken on a medium heat (400°F) until cooked through, about 20 mins. When cool, shred the meat.

3. In a food processor, purée the beans in their liq-uid so that they are creamy.

4. In a medium frying pan, cook the yellow onion about 5 mins. Stir in beans and cook until bub-bling, 1-2 mins.

5. Place a rounded spoonful of the bean mixture onto each tortilla and spread it around. Fold each tortilla over, and fry them in 2 tbsp of oil at 200°F, turning once, until golden, 3-5 mins.

6. Top each panucho with shredded lettuce, chick-en, diced tomato, and xnipec.

Refresco

Ingredients

4 cups fruit, cubed (anything Caribbean—mangoes, pineapples, oranges, tangerines, bananas; one 14 oz. can counts as one cup)

2 cups water

¼ cup sugar, or to taste

Juice of a lemon

Lime wedges, for garnish

Directions

In a blender, combine the mango and water and blend at high speed until smooth. Add sugar and lemon juice. Blend again and serve in tall glasses over ice with a wedge of lime.

Like the famous Cat, Mark Adderley was born in Cheshire, England. His early influences included C. S. Lewis and adventure books of various kinds, and his teacher once wrote on his report card, "He should go in for being an author," advice that stuck with him. He studied for some years at the University of Wales, where he became interested in medieval literature, particularly the legend of King Arthur. But it was in graduate school that he met a clever and beautiful American woman, whom he moved to the United States to marry. He has been teaching writing and literature in America ever since, and now teaches for the Via Nova Catholic Education Program in South Dakota. He is the author of a number of novels about King Arthur for adults, and originally wrote the McCracken books for his younger two children.

Made in the USA
Middletown, DE
21 December 2021

56796540R00126